P9-DMQ-450

THE KING OF THE HILL
and other stories

By the same author:

FOUR HUNDRED BILLION STARS

SECRET HARMONIES

THE KING OF THE HILL

and other stories

by

PAUL J. McAULEY

LONDON
VICTOR GOLLANCZ LTD
1991

First published in Great Britain 1991
by Victor Gollancz Ltd,
14 Henrietta Street, London WC2E 8QJ

© Paul J. McAuley, 1991

The right of Paul J. McAuley to be identified as author
of this work has been asserted by him in accordance
with the Copyright, Designs and Patents Act 1988.

ACKNOWLEDGEMENTS

'The King of the Hill' first appeared in *Interzone*, Winter
1985/6; 'Karl and the Ogre' first appeared in *Interzone*,
Spring 1988; 'Transcendence' first appeared in *Amazing*,
November 1988; 'The Temporary King' first appeared in
The Magazine of Fantasy and Science Fiction, January
1987; 'Exiles' first appeared in *Interzone*, November
1990; 'Little Ilya and Spider and Box' first appeared in
Interzone, Summer 1985; 'The Airs of Earth' first
appeared in *Amazing*, January 1986; 'The Heirs of Earth'
first appeared in *Amazing*, May 1987.

British Library Cataloguing in Publication Data
McAuley, Paul J.
  The king of the hill and other stories
  I. Title
  823.914

ISBN 0-575-05001-2

Typeset by CentraCet, Linton, Cambridge
and printed in Great Britain by
St Edmundsbury Press Ltd, Bury St Edmunds, Suffolk

Contents

The King of the Hill   *page* 7

Karl and the Ogre   29

Transcendence   47

The Temporary King   71

Exiles   99

Little Ilya and Spider and Box   121

The Airs of Earth   145

The Heirs of Earth   181

The King of the Hill

I can see the stepped, tree-circled hill, Cadbury Castle, whenever I look up from my desk. Sunlit yet ringed with darkness, haunted, brooding, singular . . . It is one of the finest examples of a fortified earthwork in England, and by its association with King Arthur, of the Knights of the Round Table, of Merlin and of the whole Matter of Britain, it is something more, a concretization of legend, a relic of a dream. And to me now, because of David, it is quite another thing altogether. An end, or a beginning.

David, my nephew, came to me after his parents died in a road accident up in war-torn Yorkshire. An American Army truck ran the bus in which they were travelling off the road, killing them and half the passengers besides. I was David's closest relative, and when he was released from hospital (he'd been on the bus too, that evening), the authorities sent him to me. A solemn, quiet, watchful boy of fourteen, scrupulously, unsettlingly polite. His red hair had been shaved around a fresh glistening scar; but he would say nothing about the accident. For a week there was a curious tenseness between us, nephew and crusty, famous bachelor uncle, but then I took him on my favourite walk, around the ditched, grassed-over defences of Cadbury Castle.

A narrow lane between tall banked hedges links the village of South Cadbury with the hill. The belt of trees around its base was tangled and bare in that season (it was a wet and blustery March day) yet so dense that the top was hidden. We went up the modern concreted path – I preferred the lesser known tractor-trail at the opposite corner of the hill, but it is always treacherous in wet weather – that climbed amongst the trees and cut through the ditches and ramparts of the old defences to the eighteen-acre field at the summit. Wind snapped in our faces as we stumped over muddy plough ridges.

Thirty years ago archaeologists had excavated a temple and a Neolithic shrine, and the post-holes of a large hall; I showed David where they were, all covered with earth again, as was the shallow depression where the gate had been. The archaeologists had found a dozen dismembered skeletons there, victims of some Roman massacre. Cadbury Castle has been defended for more than five thousand years, simple Neolithic fortifications hugely enlarged in the Iron Age, when the hill had been sculpted into its final form, added to by the Celts and then partly demolished by the conquering Romans so that the local people could not use it in the event of an uprising (but as if in recompense they had built the temple). And after the Roman withdrawal more ramparts had been built, stones piled atop the older earthworks which may have been the reality of fabled Camelot, a last stand against the invading Saxons, a last gleaming before the dark ages closed over Britain.

David endured my little lecture with a silence that was not quite sullen, simply minimally attentive; the same mood with which he mooned about the house, alone and lonely and out of place. I suggested that we walk to the summit of the ridge, the western end of which is called Arthur's Seat, and he shrugged in his yellow windbreaker as if it made no difference to him, and said nothing when I pointed out the raven which rose at our approach and flapped heavily down the slope into the trees.

At the summit we could see, across the tops of the trees, across the central plain of Somerset, once a sea and now a patchwork of fields streaked and puddled with silver floodwater, clear to the breast of Glastonbury Tor twelve miles away (the thin spire of its tower just where the nipple would begin), Avalon to Cadbury's Camelot, shadowed by mutinous clouds while we stood in windy sunlight.

"You can see everything!"

"Yes, you can."

David balled his fists inside the pockets of his windbreaker, his shoulders hunched. A defiant figure, inturned. "It isn't like Yorkshire, though. Too green and flat."

What could I say? His parents' deaths were between us. After a moment I suggested that we go back, it was cold and I wasn't as young as I'd like to be, we'd have tea.

"All right."

But at least he'd reacted to something.

As we crossed the ploughed ground we heard coming up towards us the squeal and thump of amplified pop music. David and I exchanged glances, and just as we reached the path three men came out of the line of trees below. All wore green anoraks with holstered pistols just visible at their hips, and one carried on his shoulder the enormous radio from which the music erupted. They watched us as we passed, eyes narrowed in their ruddy well-fed faces, and then one said something to his companions and they all broke into laughter. David stiffened at that but I murmured, "No need to make a scene," and was relieved when he walked on quietly. Behind us the amplified voice of a Radio Liberty announcer clawed across the summit.

As we descended between the trees, David said, "They shouldn't be allowed up there! It isn't right!"

"Ever since the National Trust bought it everyone is allowed up there, David."

"But it isn't for them. It's . . ." He couldn't explain, spat instead into the grass bordering the path.

"David, I have a friend who may be able to help, but I can't promise anything. Don't let them ruin it for you, though. There will be other days."

David simply shrugged, and I couldn't tell if he had been appeased or not.

My friend was Yeovilton's Cultural Liaison Officer, Bobby Dubois. I told him about the disturbance on Cadbury Castle when he visited me one night later that month, but he could promise nothing.

"What can I say?" he said, and opened his hands as if to show that they were empty. "I'm sorry, but we can't keep a tight rein on the personnel. They're under a lot of pressure, see."

"It's simply that I hold Cadbury Castle quite dear, and my nephew has taken a liking to it as well."

"Your nephew, sure." Dubois had met David, a brief, chilly encounter. "I guess he isn't too fond of us."

"I suppose not."

"I'll pass the word, but I don't know what good it'll do."

"Well, thank you for trying." I got up and poured us both another sherry.

Dubois watched me from the deep armchair in the flickering shadows beside the fire and nervously passed a hand over his luxuriant drooping moustache, a grooming gesture that made him look even more like a squirrel than usual. We had met because he was a music fan – by which I mean real music, of course, not the polyphonic cacophony purveyed by Radio Liberty – and when he had found out that I lived in his bailiwick he had sought me out. I knew that he was building up courage to ask his by now inevitable favour, but I said nothing, simply handing him his glass and sitting in the armchair opposite.

"Thanks," Dubois said, "I can't get enough of this stuff."

"Neither can I, these days."

He smiled, then asked, "Listen, I suppose you're not thinking of, I mean you wouldn't . . ."

He said it so timidly, as timidly as a small wild creature might reach for a hand-held crumb, that I laughed. "I'm afraid I have no plans to break my retirement."

Dubois glanced at the Steinway on the other side of the low-beamed sitting room, touched his moustache softly, tentatively. "Gee, you know it's a shame. The times you've played for me . . ."

I flexed my stiff arthritic fingers. Long as a strangler's: once I could reach two and a half octaves. They were as much use as a bundle of twigs now. "I know the difference. I'm sorry."

He shrugged and said it was always worth a try, and went on to tell me about the orchestra he was trying to bring over from Boston. "They think it's all bandits and firefights though; they don't realize how quiet it is here in the south. I thought maybe if you wrote them . . .?"

I saw his ploy then, and laughed. My weakness is that I have always underestimated people. "All right. I used to know the conductor fairly well – you know I played a season there as soloist?"

Dubois nodded eagerly. "Eighty-nine. I have a tape, Chopin's polonaises. Your Fantasia truly was magical."

"You are developing a cunning streak, Captain Dubois."

"It's kind of forced on you over here. You British never say what you mean."

"That is simply a part of our charm. Besides, look what happened when the last British government actually fulfilled all of its election promises."

"Come on, we couldn't let that go through. The Russians would be here in two weeks without our bases. We had to come here, for your own good."

I wanted to say that we were perfectly capable of making up our own minds, but it had all been said before, and I had broken the rule Dubois and I had made about never discussing politics. For all his easygoing air he was very much of the establishment view; that was why he had his job, after all. And I . . . I suppose that I was a cynic then, believing neither one side nor the other and not realizing that sitting on the fence was a luxury I could ill afford. So I changed the subject – an old man's prerogative – and we talked about music for an hour, until the lights went out.

Dubois glanced at his fantastically complicated watch. "Eight on the button. I hate to go but. Even I'm not immune to the curfew."

I went to the door to see him off. A crisp frosty night, the moon a fingernail paring crooked above Cadbury Castle. The stars hard and bright and close.

"Take care," I said, and meant it. Occasionally bandits crossed the Welsh border: it was not as quiet in the area as Dubois would have had the Boston Symphony Orchestra believe.

"Don't worry," Dubois said and gunned his motorcycle and was off.

When I went back inside I heard David moving about in the kitchen. He had lit a candle and was boiling up some milk on the camping stove: he had become used to my casual attitude towards housekeeping and eating.

"In the north we don't talk to them," he said, as soon as I came in. "How can you?"

"We both like music." But it was not quite the right answer. "I can remember when the Americans were our allies, David. I don't see what harm it does."

"What did he say about those soldiers?"

"He can't do much, you know, but he will have a word with someone, I expect."

"Well I hope they keep off anyway. You're right about it, Uncle Jimmy. It is a sort of magical place." He looked down self-consciously, showing the tiny scar amongst the cropped red hair on the left side of his skull.

"Well . . . I'm glad you like it." This sudden change of mood surprised and puzzled me. I was out of practice with young people. I liked everything settled, known, definable. As spring wore into summer I would be puzzled again and again by David's moods, nothing unusual for a teenage boy I'm sure, but novel to me. I added then, "I think it's magical too," and was relieved to see him smile when he looked up, the thinly compressed smile of my brother, who was dead.

There was, then, one interest we shared, and we often went out to Cadbury Castle together. I bought him books too, on early myth and Arthurian legends. White's *Sword in the Stone* of course, and an abridged Malory illustrated by Arthur Rackham. And Celtic and Saxon histories, a book on the archaeology of Cadbury Castle itself . . . For I was pleased to see that David had a deep and genuine interest in the place, an interest which took him out of his brooding, odd perhaps when he was at the age of burning but short-lived enthusiasms, but nonetheless real. He had made few friends at school and showed no interest in either girls or pop music – but perhaps that was because most of the latter was American, and he was constant in his loathing of anything American. I did not draw him out on this, blaming the accident and his father's vague almost romantic conception of socialism; he had been precisely the caricature socialist from whose folly the Americans claimed they had come to save us. But David's outbursts against things American were fortunately few, and he simply kept out of the way whenever Bobby Dubois came to visit me.

When, for his birthday, I took David to Tintagel Castle he did not even ask where the passes and petrol had come from, and of course they had come from Dubois. He and I had plotted deeply about the trip. So in June David and I drove south and west to Cornwall, taking the country roads where there were fewer checks, and taking our time.

David was all enthusiasm until we reached Tintagel itself. On the ramparts of the castle, overlooking a bay in which the sea lazily lapped amongst huge boulders, he told me quite firmly, "No, it isn't the place. Arthur was never here."

I teased him about his loyalty to Cadbury, but he shrugged this off, stubborn and humourless as he sometimes could be. "I mean the real Arthur," he explained, "not the one with the grail quest and the knights and the magic sword. The real Arthur's followers were kerns, and if he had a sword it would have been an ordinary Roman short sword. The rest is just a story, mostly made up of bits of older stories."

"Some of the old people in South Cadbury, you know, used to talk about the king under the hill. I remember someone told me once that when the archaeologists came his father was worried that they would wake up the king with their digging, so that he would no longer be there to defend Britain in her hour of need."

"Well, wouldn't he be back now, now we have been invaded?" David was looking out to sea, his red hair stirring in the wind.

I didn't want to hear yet another diatribe against the Americans, and I suggested that we should walk down to see Merlin's cave.

"It was nice to be brought here, Uncle Jimmy," David said, "but let's go back. There's nothing for me here."

When summer came and school broke up David spent more time than ever up on Cadbury Castle. One night, in the local pub, the man who farmed the hill came up to me and remarked, "That lad of yours gave me a real fright the other evening."

I asked about it.

"I was coming up through the woods around the hill and he came at me from out of the shadows like. Not running, I mean I didn't see him until I was almost upon him. Fair startled me. He had leaves in his hair and mud on his face like those soldiers."

"Probably just some game."

"Big lad to be playing silly buggers. I almost had a heart attack on the spot."

It was about this time that David took up with three local boys, all younger than himself. They spent a lot of time amongst the apple trees at the bottom of my garden, making bows and arrows from scratch, and David led them on expeditions that lasted long into the light summer evenings. This kind of behaviour might have worried me if it were not for his school reports: his teachers saw him as an intelligent, stable sort of lad. I supposed that he needed someone who would look up to and follow him. The lonely often need that kind of reassurance more than love. But it didn't last. Perhaps a week after I'd last seen his friends I asked David what had become of them. Why didn't they come around any more?

"They didn't understand. They thought it was all just pretend, just playing . . ."

After that he was out more than ever, coming back late in the last light, bedraggled, sweaty, and not very communicative. Most of the rest of the time he practised with his bow, peppering the garden shed until I relented and found him a proper padded straw target; secondhand of course, but it still cost a small fortune.

One day I was sitting on the patio in the sunshine when

David put up his bow and came to sit beside my chair. "Uncle Jimmy?"

"Uh-hmm?"

"Did you ever feel, well, that you *had* to do what you did?"

I put aside the not very good biography of Mahler. "It was something that I wanted to do from an early age, and luckily something I was able to do well."

"No, I didn't mean that exactly." David squinted up at me. His nose was sunburnt. "I mean, do you feel that you *had* to do it? That something made you?"

"A little, perhaps. Why, do you feel that way about something? What are you going to become?"

"That's it. I don't know exactly. It's just . . ."

But then I heard the familiar sound of Bobby Dubois' motorcycle turning into my drive. David's face hardened. "I wish he wouldn't come here."

"He's my friend, David."

But the boy simply got up and walked down the garden to start his archery practice again.

When Dubois had settled his gangling frame into the chair beside mine, he said, "I see you're training a little guerrilla."

"He made it himself, you know."

Dubois grinned. "Well, I promise not to tell Colonel Ames about it."

I had to ask who Colonel Ames was.

"Oh, our new security officer. He was brought down from York supposedly to clear up the little bit of trouble we've been having recently. Word is though he made a bad name for himself up there. Man died in custody." Dubois was silent for a moment, touching his moustache. Then he asked, "You won't spread that around. I guess it's kind of confidential."

"Mum's the word." When he looked blank I explained, "I mean I won't tell anyone. But is there trouble in this area?"

"Bad enough to cancel that tour, after I had set it all up. That's really what I came to tell you. I mean after all those letters you wrote I feel bad about it."

"I'm sorry to hear about that. It would have been quite a feather in your cap."

"Maybe when things are quieter you could write them again."

"Of course. But what has been happening?"

"Just last week for instance, some people cut the perimeter fence, garrotted a guard, set fire to a paint store. It's getting to be like the north, or Wales. Still, maybe Ames can handle it. He's a heck of a bastard, but efficient, I'll give him that. Even has us carrying guns all the time. Want to see mine?"

"Oh, I believe you!"

Dubois stretched out his long legs and put his hands on top of his crewcut head; the wicker chair creaked. "Don't be surprised if you get a lot of patrols around here from now on in, is all. Like I said, Ames is efficient, things are tightening up. Hard to believe it's gotten so bad though."

I agreed. Sitting there in the sunny tranquil garden, with butterflies flocking around the buddleia and the gently lulling knocking of David's arrows into the target, thoughts of guerrillas, of covert action and infiltration, of sabotage and night patrols, were unreal, stuff from another world.

"Well, hell," Dubois said. "It probably won't come to anything anyhow."

"But I'm sorry about the concert tour."

Dubois cheerfully shook this off and told me about his forthcoming leave and his plans for the fall, as he quaintly called autumn. Then, as abruptly as always, he decided that he had to be off. "Things to do, places to see. I'll come visit you after my furlough."

"Of course."

But I never saw him again.

That was not the beginning of it, however. If it had a beginning which I could grasp, it would be when David found the coin.

It was the end of September, in the middle of an Indian summer; the skies a clear hard blue yet the sunlight softer, less vertiginous than before. I asked David if he wanted to go for a walk and he for once agreed. We set off down the lane towards

Cadbury Castle, side by side but not speaking. A quiet day, the burr of a tractor miles away clear and small.

At least the troubles meant that we had the hill to ourselves. Five years before, on a day like that, there would have been half a dozen cars blocking the lane and people seemingly everywhere.

We climbed through the dense green woods – Dog's mercury was everywhere beneath the trees that summer – and mounted to the southern end, skirting the field of corn stubble.

After a while I asked, "Do you remember the first time I brought you here?"

"I remember the soldiers," David said. Then, "I wish it could be like this always. Peaceful. It isn't fair . . ."

I thought that he meant that soon the holidays would be over. "There'll be other summers."

"Maybe." Then David was off, racing down the grassy slope to the first setback of the earthworks and scrambling back up breathless. He flung himself on the grass and I sat beside him.

"Feel better?"

A shrug. "Up here I feel . . . free. I don't know."

He leaned back, looking into the pure sky. A lark was twittering somewhere overhead. Here. There. I was content to look out across the spread of hedged fields to where Glastonbury Tor shimmered in the heat-haze: immemorial England.

"I was thinking," David said suddenly, "about how Arthur held off the Saxons . . . until he faltered."

"And what gave him his powers?"

"Oh, the old gods." David gave me a shy sideways glance. "It isn't my idea, a lot of people have written about it, but I know it must be true. I mean the gods before the Greek and Roman gods. What were called the Titans."

"Cronus and crew," I said, remembering my classics master. That had been his phrase, but for the life of me I couldn't remember his name. "Didn't Blake write something about it?"

"Yes. Well, they were driven westwards by Zeus and so on and they came here. The land at the edge of the world, that's what the Romans called Britain. They thought there was only chaos beyond. Well, the old gods helped Arthur, you see, because his people worshipped them. The Druids held the oak sacred, and that's the symbol of Cronus's wife, Rhea. There's lots of other examples. And that's why Arthur didn't come back to fight against the Normans when they invaded, because he would have been helping the Saxons."

"It's an interesting idea."

"I think it's real, Uncle Jimmy. Arthur was only a man, you see, and he died, but the power that helped him still sleeps in the land. That's what makes it special. You said the villagers used to think Arthur was buried under this hill, but everyone knows he was buried at Glastonbury. You see, they confused the source of Arthur's power with the man. And perhaps another Arthur will gain those powers, don't you see? It's like history all over again, the invaders and the little bands fighting against them all disunited, waiting for a leader. They're mostly Welsh or Scots, you see: Celts."

I saw it as wish-fulfilment of course, and smiled and said nothing. Old age always smiles on the excesses of youth, the enthusiasms and the hot emotions, forgetting that those enthusiasms, those emotions, are real. Once I had felt like that about music, and my dream had come true, for a while. But nothing lasts.

A jetplane climbed up from the southern horizon, a glittering point that dragged its hollow roar across the perfect sky as it skimmed the fields and came on towards us. I glimpsed the yellow needlenose and the rockets slung beneath its swept-forward stubby wings and David was on his feet waving his arms in defiance before throwing himself down as it roared across the top of the hill, trees thrashing in its wake and the hot breath of its exhaust washing over us.

David shouted something and I saw the glitter in the grass just as his hand closed upon it. The jet and its noise had vanished: after a moment the lark resumed its song.

David held out a disc of unstained unworn copper, a coin. On one side a blurred profile with a wreath of ill-aligned letters above it; on the other the curt inscription with which the coiner had signed himself: GODONCADANBYRIM. *Godfrey of Cadbury*. We learned later that it was the twin of a coin which had been found years ago on the hill, and nothing at all to do with King Arthur. It had been stamped in Ethelred's reign, fifty years before the last battle was lost by Britons on British soil, on the chalk hills of Hastings.

I congratulated David on his find and asked if he was going to put the coin in a museum, but he was quite adamant that he wanted to keep it.

"Other people should have the chance to see it, David. Your name would be put beside it, on a card. Everyone would know who found it."

"I need it, Uncle Jimmy."

"I suppose that since you found it, it's yours to do with as you will. But look after it, David."

It became his good luck charm, always in his pocket, or beside him when he slept. I don't think that he showed it to anyone besides myself. It is on my desk now, as I write.

It was soon after that, after David had returned to school, that his fits began. The first took him in the middle of a class, and I remember how out of breath I was when I arrived at the school; my car was up on blocks and I had had to cycle five miles.

David was in the sickroom, lying fully-clothed on a plastic-covered couch, pale but awake and grinning sheepishly. The school nurse took me aside and said, "I'm sure it was just a faint, and then he must have been sleeping."

"How could you tell?"

"Oh, when they faint they just lie there until they come around, and their eyes are rolled up. David was like that at first, but when we put him on the couch he started to mutter, Welsh it sounded like. And his eyes were moving under the lids like when you dream. He just needs to rest, he'll be all right."

But it happened again and again as the Indian summer dissolved into rainy October. It would take him suddenly and quietly, in the middle of a meal or a sentence. The upturned eyes, the soft swooning. After a while he would begin to mutter in some throaty dialect and toss and turn as if gripped by a dream, and then, by and by, he would come around. Despite my misgivings he still insisted on his solitary expeditions, and often I would wait up long after dark, picturing him caught by a fit in the cold night; but he always came back cheerful and muddy and composed, and it seemed that exercise kept the fits at bay, for when the weather was too foul even for him they became more frequent.

The local doctor suggested that it might be something to do with the head injury David had sustained in the accident which had killed his parents, and recommended a specialist in Bristol. But at the time there was no way of taking David there. The new security officer, Colonel Ames, had issued orders restricting travel and when I wrote to him, to ask if an exception might be made in David's case, there was no reply.

A week passed, and David suffered fits on two consecutive days. By then Bobby Dubois was due back from his furlough, and I wrote to him in turn. The next day Ames appeared at my house.

It was about nine o'clock, and I was waiting for David to return from one of his expeditions, already dressing-gowned and reading by the light of an oil lantern, when someone knocked at the front door: hard, spaced, and authoritarian. I feared that something had happened to David, but when I opened the door and held up the lantern with my stiff fingers I saw that it was something worse.

The burly man in camouflage jacket and trousers, his head as shaven as any convict's, a pistol at his hip, said, "I was passing by and I thought I'd look in. I hope you don't mind, Sir James. My name is Ames. Colonel Ames."

"I see."

He laughed at my visible disbelief. "Listen, I really was in the area. We were after a couple of guerrillas. Caught one too. Would you like to see him?" He gestured towards the gate at the end of my drive, where two jeeps stood with their headlights burning, their engines ticking over.

"Not really," I said, as calmly as I could.

"I guess you wouldn't,"said Ames. And then, "Won't you invite me in?"

He did not sit but paced, almost prowled, about the room, looking at the titles on my bookshelves, running a gloved finger across the gleaming closed wing of the Steinway. A well-built man of about fifty, utterly self-assured.

After a minute I asked, "May I enquire why you have chosen to visit me at such a late hour?" Sometimes there is no other course, in the face of our conquerors' crude brashness, but to put on the stiff-backed stiff-lipped show of British outrage.

"I was wondering if you'd noticed anything unusual here. Strangers, vehicles moving around after curfew, that kind of thing."

"No. No, I haven't. Why do you ask? Is it something to do with those guerrillas you were chasing?"

"I think someone may be helping them locally, yes. Their attacks on our patrols in this area have been unusually well co-ordinated. But you say that you haven't seen anything."

"No."

"How about your nephew? I understand he roams around a lot. Maybe he can tell me something."

But David was out, and it was after the curfew. I said, "He's ill – I wrote to you about it and perhaps you remember that I mentioned that he suffers from fits. He hasn't been roaming around, as you put it, for some time now, and at the moment he is recovering from his latest episode. The doctor has insisted on absolute quiet."

Ames touched the Steinway again, perhaps considering whether it was worth pushing me on that point. But after a moment he nodded and changed the subject, telling me that he owned several of my recordings. His manner was less peremptory now, but I was still uncomfortable beneath his scrutiny.

I murmured my usual excuses that all I had now was a great career behind me, and Ames smiled. "I understand that Captain Dubois was trying to get you to play. I'd like that."

"Not very possible, I'm afraid."

"A pity. Well, it was a pleasure meeting you anyhow."

At the door he could not resist a parting shot; or perhaps it was what he had come to tell me in the first place. "Understand that when I say no, Sir James, that that is exactly what I mean. Without exception. It's no use appealing to your friend Dubois, because he has zero influence."

So Ames had intercepted my second letter. I nodded stiffly and he casually saluted and crunched off down the drive towards the jeeps.

I was working on a glass of my carefully hoarded scotch when I heard David come in. I cornered him in the hall and told him matter-of-factly about Ames' visit, and told him that I considered it too dangerous to be out after curfew from now on. I had expected a blazing argument, but he simply nodded, quite composed. It was as if he had expected it.

"I suppose it's for the best. Things are changing."

I didn't think to ask what he meant by that, and I supposed that it was an end to the matter. Of course, it was nothing of the kind.

The next day David suffered a fit just after he returned from school. I laid him out on the sitting-room sofa and soon he passed into the dream-state, sweat standing out on his forehead and his fists clenching and unclenching as he muttered hoarsely.

I sat with him until he came round, watching for an hour or more as he tossed and turned and muttered, the room darkening as the short afternoon wore out. My dead brother's features were coming into David's face, like the image which swims up at you as a photographic print develops; lean-cheeked and high-browed, a long somewhat shapeless Irish nose peppered with wide pores. Then all of a sudden his eyes opened and he smiled up at me.

"It's getting closer."

I asked him what he meant, but he was suddenly wary. "I don't know, just a dream."

I packed him off to bed and was preparing a cup of that universal English panacea, milky sugary tea, when the telephone rang. It was Dubois, sounding faint and faraway although he said that he was calling from Yeovilton. "I just got back and Ames has had my ass in the can already."

"I'm dreadfully sorry. It was stupid of me not to realize it would cause trouble for you, but I really was desperate about David and I thought you could help."

"Yeah, well that was only the half of it. Ames found out about those travel passes I worked out for you this summer. But listen, he was really only trying to scare me off, I think. There's word around here that something's coming down in your area tonight. Maybe Ames was trying to warn me off telling you."

"What sort of thing?" I was holding the telephone as if it had somehow metamorphosed into a snake. It crackled and hissed in my ear.

"Something bad. Bad. Listen, I'll be over. On my bike it'll take maybe half an hour."

"You needn't—" But the line had gone dead.

I poached an egg for David's supper and took it and the tea up to him. But I was too restless to eat myself, too restless to sit with David for long. Bad, Dubois had said, and I supposed that it was something to do with the guerrillas Ames had told me were operating in the area. But why should it involve me? I paced up and down in the sitting room and twice went out onto the drive to listen for Dubois' motorcycle.

The second time I saw a flicker at the base of Cadbury Castle's dark mound – it was dusk now, the moon a pearly haze in low fast-moving cloud. I watched the hill but the light did not come again. More than forty minutes had passed and still no sign of Dubois. Sudden irrational fear gripped me and I went to telephone his office. But the instrument was dead; not even a dial tone.

Then I remembered David and went upstairs to see how he was. He was gone.

I walked quickly down the lane towards Cadbury Castle, an electric ball, pure nervousness, spinning in my stomach as I swung my torch from side to side, half-expecting to see David huddled on the ground. My knuckles ached numbly as they always did before rain and I found it difficult to hold the torch. The moon was completely hidden now, the tall hedges on either side a chiaroscuro of shadow. And then the torch-beam yellowed, flickered, faded. Old battery. I stuffed it into my coat pocket and slowly walked on through almost complete darkness.

There is a feeling I sometimes have when I am alone and outside after dusk, a childish irrational feeling of being watched by something inimical, something that is quietly, invisibly stalking me. I had that feeling as I groped my way down the lane; my skin tingled between my shoulderblades as if in anticipation of the predator's spring.

But what came out of the darkness was a shout, a command to halt. And then a harsh blinding beam of light. I squinted into it and saw a burly figure move towards me. It was Colonel Ames.

He ordered the light to be switched off, told me to walk towards him. I was suddenly aware of rain beginning to patter down, infrequent fat drops that made a quiet pocking amongst the leaves of the hedges. When I reached him, he said silkily, "I hardly expected you to be involved, Sir James. All my reports suggested that you were harmless. Where's your friend Dubois, by the way? Yeah, I had a tap on your phone."

"I am alone, Colonel. I believe that my nephew is somewhere on the hill. He has had an attack and won't know what he is doing, so I ask you to treat him gently if you find him."

"Oh, we'll find him if he's up there, don't worry about that. That's why we're here."

My eyes had readapted to the darkness by then. Parked at the end of the lane, in the lee of the trees which leaned out from the slope of the hill, was a jeep with two soldiers lounging beside it. I faintly heard the staticky spurts of its radio.

Ames told me, "We couldn't figure out how they had been hitting our patrols in this area so accurately until we realized that someone must have been spotting them from the hill here. You can see for miles from the top on a clear night. I guess you know that. It was only on clear nights we were getting hit. Then intelligence told us to expect some action tonight. It was supposed to be a clear night too, until these clouds blew up."

I wondered about Ames' source of intelligence, then remembered the captured guerrilla and what Dubois had told me about Ames' methods of interrogation, the reason why he had been demoted to this area. "My nephew is only a boy. Surely you can't—"

"I surely can." Ames' voice was smooth and hard and cold. "Kids as young fought us in Salvador, in Nam. Younger. Kid up there with night-glasses, a CB outfit, could pin down the whole area. We found those items cached in the woods, by the way. So don't—"

He was interrupted by a call from one of the soldiers by the jeep. He caught hold of my arm and roughly bundled me with him, took the handset from the soldier and listened intently to its faint voice. "You're sure," he said, and looked at me, his gaze burning through the gloom. The voice hissed and squawked and Ames said, "Okay," and returned the handset to the soldier, telling him, "I'm going on up there. Pass the word and make sure everyone's alert."

The concrete path up the hill was a barely visible glimmer beneath the trees. As we started up it the rain began to fall more heavily and a strong wind quickened the trees; it was as if the hill were sailing off into the darkness and we were climbing amongst its straining masts.

Ames pitched his voice above the wind and the noise of the trees. "I have both paths sealed and men all around this place. All we have to do is go up and get him."

I understood that this was to be a personal victory for Ames, a way of redemption. There was something in my throat, a constriction it was painful to speak past. "David plays up here, that's all. This is some sort of ghastly coincidence."

"The fuck it is." Ames stopped walking, thrust his face close to mine. "Didn't you wonder why Dubois never showed up? He was just now found on one of those crappy little roads you have around here. They'd stretched a wire from one side to the other and he ran right into it on that hog of his. Just about took his head off. Who else would know he was coming but your kid?"

"Bobby? Surely, no." I seemed suddenly to be standing on the edge of a black slope pitching steeply down.

"You play your crappy headgames, you English, pretend everything is normal, but there's a fucking civil war going on. You won't face up to reality, that's why we're here. Well listen, your boy is up there as an accomplice to the men who killed Dubois. You want them to get away?"

I was saved from finding a reply. Somewhere above came the shocking rattle of automatic fire and then Ames was running on up the path. I followed without thought, hearing rather than seeing him as he ran, and came puffing up half a minute after he reached a pair of soldiers, heard one say something about this thing hitting a tree right by his head, someone taking off up the hill. There was a flash of torchlight and I saw for an instant the soldier's hand holding an arrow. I knew then, and the pit almost claimed me.

Ames was decisive: the soldiers were to keep their stations, he'd go on. "This storm coming up, there isn't going to be any moonlight, so keep your eyes wide."

As if to emphasize his words lightning flared and there was a dull explosion below: a bloom of ragged orange flame licked up beyond the trees.

Then Ames was running again. It was no longer pitch black, but if anything the fugitive light of the fire was worse than darkness. Half-seen trees seemed to leap at me, their branches writhing, as I followed Ames, and once again I felt that I was being stalked. The flickering darkness amongst the trees could have held anything.

When I left the shelter of the trees the rain hit with a thousand cold needles, soaking me through in a moment. I stopped, absolutely out of breath, my legs quivering. I was used to strolling, not running, up that path.

Ames came back to me, and I shouted that we would never find anyone in this.

"Your boy's friends found the goddamned jeep!"

"That was lightning. They shouldn't have parked near the trees. If we go up there we could be struck ourselves."

"You know that kid. Get him to come quietly and I promise he won't be hurt." He grabbed my arm and more or less hauled me up the path.

As we climbed lightning cracked the dark streaming clouds again and again, as if we were mounting an auditorium lit by flashbulbs. When we reached the top the greatest bolt so far burst directly overhead, and I glimpsed David halfway across the huge field, blurred by drifting rain, an arrow fitted in his half-raised bow. Then the light was gone and Ames' pistol made its own puny thunder and lightning beside my ear.

Sometimes we act despite ourselves. I threw myself at Ames and more by luck than judgement clawed the pistol from his hand. But I couldn't fit my stiff fingers around its trigger and as I flung it away he was on top of me, cursing hard and pounding me with his fists. My heavy coat, made heavier by the rain, protected me from the worst, but one blow caught the side of my head and for a moment I passed out.

And came to as thunder rolled overhead, glimpsed Ames running hard towards David a moment before lightning took him, blue-white fire that instantly obliterated his shadow, a vast tree of jagged light that raked every corner of the sky. Then it was gone, and thunder smashed down.

I remember little more. Ozone seared my throat and a sensation as of pinpricks covered every inch of my body. I was lying in darkness, quiet rain, no longer the downpour of the storm, only rain, falling on the grass all around. I felt rather than saw David as he stooped over me.

"I have to go now, Uncle Jimmy. I have to. It's what I was born for, don't you see? But look after this for me, I don't need it now."

I may have dreamed it. But later, when the soldiers had finished questioning me and had satisfied themselves that I could tell them nothing coherent, when I had returned home and was alone once more, I found the coin, David's good luck piece, in one of my pockets. The blurred profile: the enigmatic mocking inscription.

I write this four years after the event, in the middle of a time of changes, a time of war. The guerrillas finally arose from their scattered outposts this spring; now it is September, and they have conquered as far west as Bristol, even now lay siege to Oxford. Every day a dozen or so refugees trickle into the camp where I work, bringing rumours that soon the guerrillas will march on London. And rumours too of their leader, conflicting and various to be sure, yet all agree that he is very young. And one woman who claimed to have seen him in the ruins of Birmingham told me that he was red-haired.

I am afraid. Not of the troubles – I have had my life – but for what may come when they are over. If David was right, and the old gods have arisen to defend their island, what will they want after their victory? The needs of men and gods so rarely coincide. If David was raised up by them, then surely the accident which killed his parents was a part of their plan. And the arthritis which ended my career and led to my retirement in the shadow of Cadbury Castle, and Bobby Dubois' murder . . . These are bitter thoughts.

I can only hope that David has wisdom as well as strength of purpose. I can only hope that the gods will again sink far beyond the knowledge of men when they are satisfied that the danger is past, and fade from our history as a troubling dream fades when we awake.

Karl and the Ogre

The three hunters, Karl and Shem and Anaxander, picked up the ogre's trail only a day after they had left the village and begun to follow the river back along its course to the spot where the unicorn had been killed, deep in the folded foothills of the Berkshires. Steeply sloping woods cluttered with ferns and mossy boulders. Slim trees, beech and sugar maple, leaning every which way in hot green light. June, the sky a blank blue. They'd gone down to the water to refill their bottles, and there, in a little embayment between white boulders tumbled by snowmelt floods, Karl found the ogre's bootprints in wet gravel at the river's edge.

A gangling blond lad of twenty summers, Karl wiped sweat from his eyes as he stared down at the prints – flat, intagliated with the waffle pattern of oldtime shoes – and felt no elation. After a moment he called over the others.

Anaxander nervously shook black, elflocked hair from his eyes and barely glanced at the prints before dancing away, trailing a high happy babble, *ulu-la-ulu-la-la*, then spinning around and cocking his head to listen to the trill of some bird in the woods that rose above the river. Meanwhile, Shem put his hands on the knees of his jeans and puzzled over the sign: poor, slow, patient Shem. He'd been the best hunter of all, Karl's mother had said, before the transgression which had brought down the changelings' anger. They had broken the edge of his intelligence then, leaving only a dog's dull unquestioning loyalty. Karl had never learnt what Shem had done; none of the hunters liked to talk about it, not even his often outspoken mother – and now she was gone, sent by the grim changeling who had charge of the hunters' guild to track down the last of the ogres in the rainy forests of the North Pacific coast.

Karl said impatiently, "Not such a big one this time. My weight or maybe a little less."

". . . Maybe," Shem said at last, and straightened, squinting against the sundazzle that salted the swift-running river. Sweat shone on the dappled horseshoe of baldness that pushed into his red hair. He said, "Let it be clean this time, boy. None of the talk. Just do it."

"Talking about the oldtime doesn't harm," Karl said, smiling, sure in his power over the older man.

". . . Maybe. I don't know, boy."

Karl swatted at a mosquito. "There's an undine in this river, right? Worth calling up, I guess."

"I guess," Shem said, while Anaxander pulled the little wooden pipe from his belt and trilled the notes of the birdsong he'd just heard.

Squatting in hot sunlight, Karl laboriously scratched the necessary signs on a heavy granite pebble with his bodkin, then straightened and lobbed the stone out into the central current. Immediately, the glass-green water there boiled in white foam. An arm as long as Karl was tall broke surface, huge hand spread to show the membranes looped between the fingers; and each finger tipped with a claw curved like the thorn of a rose. Then her inhuman face, hair tangled like waterweed about it; then her shoulders and breasts, as smooth and white as the boulders of the shore. Water spraying from the gill-slits in her neck, the undine sculled in the current, turning to face the hunters.

But she had little to tell them. Yes, she said in answer to Karl's questions, yes, the ogre had drunk the water of the river that morning, just after dawn. And yes, there had been only one creature. But when it had drunk its fill, it had turned and gone up the hillside, and the undine knew no more of it. Karl thanked her and she sank back, hair floating out from her face as water closed over it and she dissolved into her element.

Then there was only the sound of the river and the high piping of the birds in the green woods.

"Come on," Karl said, picking up his blanket-roll. "There are bound to be tracks through the undergrowth up there – the dirt's so wet you can kick a spring out of it with your heel. What is it, Ax?"

Anaxander was pointing across the river. Karl shaded his eyes and saw a deer step daintily over a spit of gravel, then lower its head and drink.

"I see it," Karl said, "but it's on the wrong side. I could put an arrow in it, sure, but I'm not swimming across to get it, and none of us can walk on water. Or can you, Ax, huh?"

Shem said hoarsely and urgently, "They said it was not allowed to kill anything but the ogre. You remember, boy, remember the cow. Ready for us when we return. Not allowed, here."

The placid Jersey cow, her long-lashed eyes looking trustingly at the village slaughterer as he placed a hand on her white muzzle. Her abrupt sideways collapse. Karl said bitterly, "You'd think we'd be free of their damned rules up here!"

Shem shrugged; Anaxander piped a fragment of the tune which the girl had sung. Karl reddened and plunged his fists into the pockets of his long cotton coat. No use scolding the idiot, he probably didn't mean anything by it. Although you were never sure, never really sure. Anaxander was an idiot, but he was also a changeling. You never really knew what went on behind those clear blue eyes. "Come on," Karl said, after a moment. "Still a long stretch before sunset. The damn ogre might even have its lair near, huh? So put that pipe away, Ax. It might hear."

Shem glanced at Karl, and the boy, his ears beginning to burn, turned and started off up the slope beneath the trees. But as he cast about for signs of the ogre's passage – moss scraped from the ground, a bent twig, a fresh-turned pebble – he could not help remembering the girl. The changeling girl as she had come along the shore of the lake with the basket resting on the swell of one hip, butterflies dancing about her long hair in the sunlight. Karl remembered her with angry helplessness mixed with loathing. No. She was not, never would be, for the likes of him.

They had arrived at the village, Karl and Shem and Anaxander, around noon two days before, their horses tired and fidgety in the heat. There was a thorn fence twice the height of a man, its barbs as hard and as sharp as tempered iron, and so thick that the gate, barred and bolted, stood at the end of a kind of tunnel. The three hunters had to wait outside until the sun sank to its last quarter before the village began to wake and the kobold which guarded the gate would let them in. Karl, thirsty and with a thick head from sleeping in the heat, followed the shambling gatekeeper with the others, leading their horses over close-cropped turf. Sheep scattered from their path.

The village stood beyond fenced hay meadows, near the shore of a lake that reflected the dark trees encircling it: a huddle of whitewashed stone cottages each in its own garden and thatched with reeds, backed by strips of vegetable gardens and white-fenced paddocks where horses grazed. The three hunters were led away from this to a big barn with a hex-eye painted on one side like a target, which stood next to a rambling single-storey house.

These belonged to the village slaughterer, of course, a gnarled, bird-like man who dismissed the kobold and took charge of the hunters, showing them into the barn and telling them to wait for the village council. The hunters watered and brushed down their horses; then, while Anaxander and Shem sprawled on clean straw and slept again, Karl sat just inside the barn's big, square door, fretting at the delay even though he should by now have become used to the changelings' disdain.

Beyond the barn, a grassy slope ran down to the edge of the lake. Presently, a girl walked down from the slaughterer's house with a wooden bucket, and Karl watched as she stooped to fill it, and watched her walk back, her soft leather kilt flapping at her plump calves, sunlight shimmering on her cotton jerkin, on her long flowing hair and the scraps of colour which danced about it. Then she was inside the house, the door closed. Karl saw that, further along the shore, the deputation of the village council was making its way towards the barn.

Karl rose and shook the stiffness from his legs, roused Shem and Anaxander. Blue eyes shining mischievously, the changeling pranced about the two men, blowing shrill dissonances on his pipe; Karl managed to grab his arm and push him forward into the sunlight just as the villagers halted outside.

At first glance the half dozen men and women were unremarkable, but something about their bearing, a pure, calm certainty, always intimidated Karl, so that he became uncomfortably aware of his shirt sticking to his shoulderblades, the dirt under his fingernails, the rank smell of his own sweat mingled with that of his horse. Their spokesman, a plump man of fifty or so, started off by addressing Anaxander, and when Karl pointed out the error simply shrugged and said to the idiot with solemn courtesy, "I am sorry, brother."

Karl said, "He doesn't understand much of anything except music."

"He understands," one of the women said, eyeing Karl and Shem with displeasure.

And so as usual it began badly, Karl angry yet at the same time more afraid than he cared to admit – for any one of the changelings, however homely their appearance, could have twisted him inside out as easily as snap a pod of peas. At least it was a straightforward task. The spokesman explained that the village had long suspected that at least one ogre survived in the hills beyond the lake, and that suspicion had been confirmed when a freshly killed unicorn had been found there. Karl guessed that the villagers had in fact tolerated the creature for some time; ogres were often the source of a multitude of minor nuisances around changeling villages, either from genuine hatred, or foolishness, or simple bravado, rarely the agent of a single outrage. Easier to ignore such trespasses than cause the kind of upset a hunt involved, raising the guilt of the deaths of all the people of the oldtime: but the murder of a sacred creature could not be ignored.

So he said, "Unicorn, huh? Well now. How long ago was that?"

"Twelve days."

Karl considered, working out the time it had taken to organize this hunt, the time they had taken to ride out here. He said, "Why did you wait two days or more before notifying our guild? The thing could have left the area by now."

"There was, as now, a reshaping. That could not be disturbed." The plump man's gaze was remote and unfathomable, without trace of guilt. As always, Karl was made to feel that, somehow, he was in the wrong; he fumbled through the rest of the routine, the questions about when and where, and was relieved when the changelings took their leave.

Later, the girl Karl had seen filling her water-bucket came up to the barn, a basket balanced on an outthrust hip: a flagon of cider, a ripe cheese, bread, honey. Karl thanked her, then said impulsively, "Your father is the slaughterer, right? I guess we have something in common."

The girl lowered her gaze, and Karl was able to study her round, pretty face. Her long hair had been braided over one shoulder. A butterfly sat above the swell one of her small breasts made in her cotton jerkin, wings pressed upright like praying hands; others, he noticed, fluttered in the warm shadows of the barn. She said, "You are surely too young to be a hunter. I have heard it said that they are not allowed children."

It was true, of course, and Karl blushed to be reminded of his singular birth. The changelings put something in the food of the Hunter Towns, it was said, or in the water, or in the very air, some oldtime poison that stopped women conceiving. Away from the Hunter Towns the poison wore off, so hunting parties consisted only of men or of women; but sometimes hunting parties would meet in the wilderness, by accident or design. In one of her more drunken moments before she had left for the North Pacific coast, Karl's mother had told him that his father could have been any one of three men: he had hated her for that. Now, he told the girl boastfully, "I've been a hunter five years now, killed eleven ogres." He realized at once that it was the wrong thing to say, and quickly added, "You mustn't be frightened of me. I've come to help your village."

"Oh, I'm not at all afraid of you." Her smile was the merest upcurving of the ends of her delicious lips. How old was she? Fifteen? Sixteen? All of Karl's drinking companions were at least as old as his mother or Shem, as were his few lovers and fewer confidants. He had the briefest fantasy of running off with the girl, finding a place in the wilderness to live as the ogres did. Hunters did that sometimes, and were hunted down like ogres for it. And then Anaxander pranced over, blowing fragments of some remembered melody through his little pipe, and the girl shied.

"Don't worry," Karl said. "He's harmless too, really he is."

"But why is the brother with you?"

"He's one of you, all right, but stupid, you understand? The brain damaged. All he understands is music; any tune he hears he can play right back like one of the oldtime machines."

The girl drew herself up and Karl was suddenly afraid. Her gaze was bright and imperious, like a sudden blade of light in the dim barn. Butterflies swirled around her head like multicoloured flakes of flame. She said, "You must not talk of such things."

"I didn't mean—"

"I must go now."

"I'm sorry," Karl said. "I didn't mean to upset you."

"Really, I must go." Was her gaze softer? "My father and mother must have an early supper. There is a change, this night."

"What are they doing to the world this time?"

"It's not our place to know."

And then she was hurrying away over grass striped with lengthening shadows. And she sang as she went, some atonal complex chant sung in a high clear voice that touched something in Karl even though he understood it not at all.

*

And now, as the hunters followed the ogre's trail through the steeply slanting forest, Anaxander pipingly played fragments of the girl's song, mixed in with scraps and snatches of other remembered melodies, and Karl mumbled at the edges of his memory of her, trying not to think of the terrible thing which had happened later. No, she wasn't for him.

At least the trail was easy to follow. Rather than keep to the clumps of rock which thrust through the rich mould of the forest floor, the ogre had followed a winding path over the soft ground between. It was almost too easy, but then all ogres were old, now. Karl's mother had regaled him with tales of desperate fights and hard tracking in the old days, and if even half those stories had been true, those ogres which remained were poor relics indeed. The last one Karl had helped dispatch had been quite without speech, a baby no doubt when it had all changed, grown wild in the years since, no more than a frightened animal. It had been a long time since Karl had learnt anything new about the oldtime, and that had been from the babblings of an arthritic half-crazed crone to whom Shem's knife had been a blessing.

They were high above the river now, could see an oldtime road like a broken-backed snake amongst the trees on the other side. Karl tried to imagine what it had been like, with *autos* roaring along in clouds of fire and smoke – that at least was something all the ogres agreed on, the terror and majesty of the oldtime roads . . . Shem had stopped, was sniffing the air. After a moment Karl caught a trace of the scent, raw and foul in the hot air.

"Spiders," Shem said.

They went on cautiously, and soon Karl saw filthy grey webs swagged from tree to tree ahead, glimpsed a dark shifting movement within their shadows. He shivered. "I wonder what they were thinking of, bringing those things into the world."

Shem wiped sweat from his balding pate and said, slowly and seriously, "Everything has its purpose. We aren't to understand it."

"Pity they couldn't dream up something useful, something that would hunt down ogres."

"They have us," Shem said after a moment.

"I guess so, and what would we do if we didn't have hunting? I'd hate to be on one of those labour gangs pulling down the old buildings." Although sometimes Karl wondered just what was left in the miles of brick and concrete the gangs were slowly turning back into the earth. He sighed and settled his blanket-roll more comfortably. "Well, it won't have gone through those webs, anyhow. Spiders'll eat an ogre as happily as you and me, or you, Ax! Don't get too close now! Let's look around."

After only a brief search Shem gave a low call and Karl crossed to him, jeans brushing through ferns. The older man pointed to the freshly broken sapling, the waffleprint beyond.

Karl flapped at the midges which danced around his head. "That's strange," he said. "The ogre is pretty lightfooted, but here it's broken this sapling like it deliberately stepped on it. As if it wants us to follow it."

"Stupid, maybe," Shem suggested. "Killed the unicorn, after all."

"That was dumb, not stupid. There's a difference. We'll go easy, you think? Watch every step. You hear, Ax?"

Grinning broadly, the idiot changeling shook hair from his white forehead.

There were other signs as they climbed the slope, slashed branches, red earth scraped free of moss. Karl, following Shem's example, cut a sturdy sapling and used it as a staff to probe before him, but it was Anaxander who sensed the trap, where the ogre's trail passed between two lichenous outcrops of rock.

The point of Karl's staff sank deep in the litter of broken branches there, and he kicked them aside. Beneath was a freshly dug pit, shallow and perhaps an arm's-breadth wide, twice as long. A dozen or more sharp-pointed stakes were set at its bottom, whittled points smeared with shit.

Shem looked at this for a long time. "Survivalists used this trick, long time ago now. All dead I thought. They wanted to fight, not hide. Kids left arsenals by their parents, see. I don't know . . ."

Anaxander was watching them with wide anxious eyes, and Karl said, "Don't worry, Ax, it's long gone. This trap, see, it hoped to catch us."

Shem scratched his stubbled chin.

"Now we go real slow," Karl told them.

But there were no more traps. The ogre's tracks, mostly keeping to a narrow deer-trail that wound amongst the trees, led on up the slope, crossed here and there by little streams. Karl's boots kept slipping on the skim of moss and liverwort over the wet clay. Here and there bushes with dark leaves were in flower, each small white star-shaped bloom as intense as an epiphany in the green shade. Then the trees gave out to scrub and grass and at last the three hunters gained the windy crest of the ridge, saw other ridges rolling away beneath the blue sky. Far out a small shape was crossing the sky from east to west. Shading his eyes, Karl could just see that it was a chariot pulled by a phalanx of huge birds, and he felt a pang of empty jealousy: there was some changeling Lord or Lady and here he was, slogging through the muck of the world.

The ogre had left a trampled track through the long dry grass. The hunters followed it down the reverse slope, and had not gone far into the trees when they reached the edge of a clearing where an oldtime ruin sagged in a shaft of sunlight, the collapsed shell of a wooden house beside a little brook shaded by dense ferns. There was a ragged black hole at the base of the ruin, a little apron of earth stamped flat in front of it; off to one side was a pile of blackened bones and other rubbish.

By now the three hunters had established a routine; rather than try to smoke out the ogre, it was safer (even if tedious) to wait for it to emerge of its own accord. Shem crept around to the back of the ruin and found a hiding place in a clump of ferns by the brook while Karl and Anaxander lay in wait in front, watching the ragged entrance to the lair. Once, Anaxander made to draw out his pipe and Karl swatted the idiot's hand away, whispered to him to be quiet and still. The changeling looked at him with wide eyes, then rolled over to look up through the trees, his lips moving as he mumbled some melody or other. Unwittingly, as he waited, Karl's mind circled about the memory of the girl in the village, and of what had happened on that night, the night of the reshaping.

He had taken a hunk of bread from the food she had left, poured himself a hefty shot of cider and retreated into the depths of the barn to brood on the day's small humiliations. And must have fallen asleep, for he woke with hazy light drifting through the doorway, the warm night beyond. Shem and Anaxander snored at different pitches. His muscles stiff from the day's ride, Karl stepped to the doorway. The air seemed to tingle with anticipation, small static discharges, and he remembered what the girl had said: a change.

Outside, the moon rode like a bruised baleful eye in green and yellow scarves of light which washed the whole sky. The little lights of the village shone around the swerve of the lake shore like stars settled to earth. Although the night air was warm, Karl shivered, wondering what was being worked on the world, what new thing was being brought into it or what was being changed, by the collective will of the changelings operating down in the whirl of elementary particles where *what is* blurs and widens into a myriad possibilities.

The lights of the slaughterer's house were also lit, and by their spilled glow Karl saw a pale shape on the grass near the edge of the water. The girl. His heart beating quickly and lightly, he walked down to her. Halfway there all the lights of the village and the lights behind him went off, but he was able to see well enough by moonlight and the cold flickerings of the aurora.

The girl sat crosslegged, leaning over the cradle of her knees. She didn't seem to be breathing.

Karl said, "I couldn't sleep either." There was no reply. When he knelt beside her he saw the whites of her eyes showing under her half-closed lids. "Hey," he said softly, and dared to touch her shoulder.

She shuddered, and in the same instant Karl felt a kind of contracting coldness over his whole skin. The change. The girl's mouth hung open, and he thought that he saw her tongue flick out. No, whatever it was, was like a pair of little whips. Then the dusty wings broke free of her lips and the fat moth flutteringly fell.

The girl was making a kind of hollow gargling. Something else was pushing past her lips with a slow heaving motion.

Karl fled, falling once and smearing grass and dirt on the knees of his jeans, getting more dirt under his fingernails as he pulled himself up and ran on. In the stuffy, scratchy heat of the barn, he lay awake a long time, seeing over and over the moth push out of her mouth into the world. And now, sprawled in dusty fern fronds, watching the entrance to the ogre's lair, he shivered despite the warm air at the memory, a queer cold feeling in the pit of his stomach. His mother had been right when she had said, as she so often did, that the changelings were not human.

The sun sank lower, brushing the top of the fern clump where Shem hid with brassy light. At last, Karl saw a stirring in the ragged hole at the base of the ruins and the ogre poked out its shaggy head, pausing as if to sniff the air before slowly and painfully crawling into the open. At once Karl stood, and after a moment Anaxander sprang up too, trembling lightly. The ogre brought up its rifle and there was the faintest click. "Damn," it said in a high cracked voice, and Shem launched himself from his concealment and knocked it into the dirt.

It was a woman, of course. Karl had guessed as much from the unicorn's murder. An old, scrawny woman, wrapped in a kind of cloak of badly tanned deerhide over ragged, faded oldtime jeans and workshirt, more darns than cloth, her hair tangled in greasy ropes. But she could talk, and once she realized that she wasn't going to be killed straight away she grew garrulous, told Karl that the unicorn had chased right after her to lay its great golden horn in her lap. That was when she had cut its throat.

The wrinkles on her face rearranged themselves around her smile. "Thought it was going to spear me straight off."

"It would have, if you hadn't been . . . well." Karl felt a cold clear elation, could only just control his eagerness to press out all that this creature knew.

"A virgin, oh yes! Never was anything but a few of us girls out here, heh heh." Then she frowned and said, "I hate those things they make. Hate them."

She needed only a little prompting from Karl to yield up her life story. Her name was Liza Jane Howard, she said, and she had lived here most of her life. "When the change came Pappy hid me here. He was a biologist, knew he was dying, everyone past puberty was dying, but didn't know the superbrights had done it. I didn't either, for the longest time. Changed the bacteria in the guts, see, so they killed any adult. After a couple of years it was all over, and then I guess they changed the bacteria back, so they could grow up, huh?" Karl nodded. He already knew this much from his brief interrogations of the other ogres he had helped to track down. "I stayed up here," she said, her eyes unfocused, that time of winnowing closer to her than the blue evening. "Kept to myself, that's how I survived. Oh, I'd talk to a few like me, but never let them know where I lived. Had a little girl here once, in the early days, sick little thing, died of pneumonia inside a month. Never did learn her name, suppose it was a blessing, huh? Haven't seen anyone for a couple of years now. Soon we'll all be gone and there'll be nothing but the superbrights."

"Those are the changelings," Karl prompted.

"You don't know, boy? See, back in the old days there was a way of enhancing a baby's intelligence before it was born, all the rich people had it done. But they didn't know just how much they changed those damned kids until the kids started changing the world. All the adults going was the first of it." She peered at Karl. "You didn't know?"

"Not the whole story." His mother had never taught him any history; but his mother had only been a baby when it had happened, an ordinary baby.

On the other side of the clearing, Shem coughed and spat, as always disapproving of this talk, wanting to finish the job. Anaxander scuffed at the grass, watching the ogre with mingled fear and fascination.

She said, "Wonder I stayed alive as long as I did, with all the changes going on. Waking up and finding giant *spiders* hung in the trees, or little dragons hiding under stones, whistling like kettles. And the wolves came back, never sure if that was natural or their working. Heh. Soon enough they'll have changed the world right out of the goddamn universe, then where'll you be, eh boy? You ever think about what'll happen when you hunt the last of us down?"

Karl remembered the cow killed in readiness for their return, the trusting way it had followed the slaughterer, its sudden unstrung collapse at the touch of his hand.

The ogre cackled. "Know why they changed it the way they did? You ever read oldtime books? Pappy left me with thousands."

Karl couldn't read, but he had heard about books from one or two of the ogres. His curiosity tingled under his entire skin. He had never before met an ogre who knew so much about the way things were before it changed.

"You come inside, boy. I'll show you," she said. "Show you where it all comes from."

"Sure, okay."

Shem stood, hand on the sheathed knife at his hip. "Listen, boy, that's a bad idea, a crazy idea."

"She can't hurt me," Karl said angrily. He had to know, had to see. Anaxander looked at him, looked at Shem, eyes wide. Karl said to the idiot, "It's okay, isn't it, Ax?" But the idiot looked away indifferently.

"I haven't a tooth left in my head," the ogre said, "and you've got my rifle there. I just want to show him how it was."

Shem pressed his hands over his ears, shook his head.

"Come on," Karl said, and pushed the ogre towards the ragged hole.

It stank inside, a mixture of old urine and sweat and hot

tallow from the candles which burned in niches in the crumbling brick walls. A pile of rotting cloth made a kind of nest; more covered the floor, tearing beneath Karl's boots. He had to stoop beneath the cobwebbed ceiling. Muttering, the ogre rummaged through a pile of rubbish, disturbing insects which skittered away into shadow. At last she held up something big and square, opened it to show still-bright pictures. "See," she said, riffling the pages in front of Karl's face, "see?"

The pictures didn't move, as one ogre had told Karl, but still they held his entire attention: drawings of dragons, of griffins, of a unicorn with delicate hoof raised in some impossible leafy bower, of a village—he grabbed the book, peered at it in the uncertain candlelight. A cluster of white, thatched cottages surrounded by a high thorn fence, in a clearing in a dark forest. "What is this?" he said. He couldn't understand how an oldtime book could contain images of the here-and-now.

The ogre cackled, shadows deep in the lines of her face. "A children's book. Understand? Something made for children to look at, tales of made-up places to entertain them. When they changed the world, the superbrights were only children, the oldest my age back then. Eight, I think. Hard to remember. Most much younger. This was all they knew, so this was how the world was changed. All out of fairytale books. Only it's real now, Utopia built on the bones of almost everyone who lived back then. Look at that, let me show you something else."

While she rummaged, Karl turned damp, mottled pages, blinking at the fantastic illustrations of the familiar. The ogre turned to him again, and he saw that she held a little pistol. Something in him relaxed. He had been expecting some such trick.

"My damn rifle might not have worked," she said calmly, "but this'll do for you and your friends. No offence."

The click as the hammer fell was small in the dank space. No other sound.

Karl said gently, "It's Anaxander. He's an idiot, but he's also a changeling. He has a power which stops weapons working against him or against his friends. He doesn't even have to think about it: it's like blinking."

The ogre screeched in rage and threw the pistol at Karl. He ducked and it clattered against brick as she rushed past, scrabbled through the entrance hole. Then silence. One by one the candles resumed their level burning. Karl calmly searched for the pistol and tucked it in his waistband, then crawled outside. Shem stood over the ogre's pitifully thin body, licking blood from the blade of his knife.

Much to Shem's disgust, Karl insisted on burying the body. The older man sat on a boulder as Karl scooped out dirt with a board and said sulkily, "Won't do any good. Wolves will come and dig it up."

Karl furiously attacked the earth and didn't reply. By the time he had finished the evening light was almost gone. Sweating, he rolled the ogre's body into the hole, kicked dirt on top of it, stamped it down. Shem watched impassively; Anaxander idly piped fragments of melody. Karl took a pebble and scratched a spell on it, tossed it into the lair. Flame licked out instantly. The only conjurations he'd been taught were those which called up elementals, but they were enough.

Anaxander leading (glancing back now and then to see the shapes the smoke made as it rolled into the sky), the three hunters climbed through the forest. When they came out of the trees at the crest of the ridge they saw that the sky was alive with slowly writhing banners of light and Anaxander pointed, grinning delightedly. As they went on the changeling took out his pipe and played a slow rolling melody in solemn celebration of the change.

Shem said to Karl, his voice low, "Throw it away, boy."

Automatically, Karl's hand went to the pistol tucked in his belt.

"Won't do you no good. If *he*—" Shem pointed at the idiot who pipingly paraded ahead of them—"can stop oldtime things working, any of them can, I should know, huh?"

"That's just what they did to you talking."

"Maybe so. Can't see how I'd tell. Don't want to see you in trouble, boy, is all."

"What will happen?" Karl cried out. "What will happen when they don't need us anymore?"

Shem shrugged. Further down the trail Anaxander looked around, green eyes luminous, then went on, playing his slow tune. Karl hefted the pistol, real as any unicorn or dragon, then abruptly threw it far into the undergrowth. The loss didn't matter. He knew now that a part of the oldtime lived still, would always live, in the fabulous conjured beasts, in the very stones, white as bone, of the cottages of the little village by the lake, of all the little villages of the changed world.

"Come on, boy," Shem said, and Karl hurried to catch up with him. Together, they followed the changeling down into darkness.

Transcendence

The little death, the black instant when his mind was neither in his body nor in the Bronovski circuits of the surveyor, passed. Like a hand pushing into a glove, as a man rushes incontinently into his lover's embrace, Lucian Singer entered into full link. Hell poured into his senses.

He checked that the machine's coating nozzles were flowing and executed a three hundred and sixty degree scan to orientate himself. Silicon crystal-forms, sprung from seed-matrices in the friable soil, shattered under his treads. No more alive than viruses, they grew, or so Singer believed, in response to the fluoro-silicones shed by the surveyor. Lines of them marked eroding tracks in the floor of the sinuous fault-valley. On either side, slopes littered with shattered rocks of all sizes bellied up, distorted by the jelly-like air. Other senses informed Singer that the cloudbase was at 48 kilometres, the temperature here in the highlands of Ishtar Terra was 710 degrees centigrade, the wind was gusting to eighty kilometres an hour: comparatively, a mild spring zephyr. Through the dull red murk above, lightning flickered in constant delicate filigrees, and the sun was a belt of faint light that girdled the horizon, concentrated in one place like a bleary eye.

Lucian Singer unfolded his extensors. It was time to begin work, for all that the rescue mission had inserted itself in orbit and was closing on his station. He was determined to prove that he was as good as the new operator, the cyborg brain-in-a-box. *Better*. This was his world.

He'd been working a low cliff for two weeks now, following thin fossiliferous seams of shale a centimetre at a time, visual sensors popping in and out of full magnification so as not to miss anything. Once exposed, the fossils corroded quickly, and he worked in a continual mist of the same short-chain fluorosilicones which coated and protected the surveyor. Even so, the tiny delicate spirals and cones and ridged rods lasted no more than a few minutes, and he flipped each into the analyser port for holography and spat it out even as he was prying away another crumbling layer.

The surveyor was tireless; Singer's mind was not. Every half an hour he retracted the extensors and moved back, treads gripping flaking shards. It was during one of these breaks, every sense drinking in the world he had come to love in his exile, that he saw a line of violet light scratch across the louring sky. Ionization trail! Pushing his optical sensors to their extreme limit, he glimpsed a sphere wrapped in glowing plasma, lost it in the warping air. Then it was overhead, the heatshield tumbling away from a broad-based delivery capsule as a huge silver parachute blossomed above. Singer tracked it until it vanished. Theoretically, the same trick of refraction which distorted and fixed the sun should have made any part of the planet visible, a bowl rising to infinity; in fact, lightscattering in the dense atmosphere limited vision to half a dozen kilometres. But the surveyor's computer had plotted enough of the trajectory to be able to calculate the approximate place of impact: less than twenty kilometres to the east, out on the lava plain.

Raped, Singer thought angrily, and initiated the procedure that would send his mind back into his body. Amid a rising black hum, Venus vanished.

After the accident which had killed his two companions and stranded him, it had taken two years to put a rescue mission together, and another six months, following a long, slow, energy-conservative Hohmann orbit, for the ship to reach Venus. After so long, Singer had become accustomed to solitude, and despite Alice Rackham's peptalks and, latterly, the brief conversations with his rescuers (he had once trained for a year with the commander, Bobby Sarowitz, but that mission had been scrubbed), the thought of other people in orbit around Venus was as distasteful and strange as contemplating a wife's infidelity. As for someone else working on the surface . . . in the end, he'd taken to switching off whenever Rackham raised the subject, and by and by she'd taken the hint.

But although celestial mechanics grind slowly, their consequences are inevitable. The rescue mission had neatly inserted into orbit two days ago, and in one more they would rendezvous with Singer's ramshackle station. He had assumed that they would wait before sending the cyborg's machine down, but had never talked about it with them – hence his sense of outraged betrayal when he had seen the ionization track.

Blackness, as the analogue of the electrical and chemical flux of his mind was played back into his brain and new memories transcribed. And then the little constellations of telltales above the couch which cradled his body and kept its automatic functions ticking over while he was downlink. Singer pushed back his dreadlocked hair and unhooked the big master cable from the socket at the back of his neck, punched the buckle release and with an economical push of his wasted legs arrowed neatly through the hatch into the communications shack.

It took several minutes for his signal to reach Earth, several more for the JPL computers to hunt down Dr Alice Rackham. Singer sipped orange juice from a squeeze bag, the cold righteous anger of the slighted, the unjustly wounded, building like a static charge in his head. When the screen finally cleared, he said without preliminaries, "You didn't tell me that she was going down to the surface today. That's my area, at least! I've explored it over and over; there's nothing left for her to discover."

Rackham was lounging on a couch in her yard, her face half-hidden by sunglasses. During the lag while Singer's accusations crawled at lightspeed to Earth, were channelled through the JPL net, and Rackham's reply came crawling back, each watched the other steadfastly, a polite convention that had solidified into habit. Rackham's glittering mask was unsettling, insectile, giving nothing away. Finally, she said, "We chose that area of Ishtar Terra precisely because you *have* explored it. You should look at your files more often, Lucian: they contain a full update. Lord knows you won't talk to me about it."

It was true, but he wouldn't admit it. And he hadn't looked at his files because ever since the rescue mission had left Earth orbit they had been filled to overflowing: appeals from UFO-cultists to expose the "official lie" that Venus was a superheated hell; jargon-riddled letters from space-freaks; political appeals; a list of projects in need of an advertising figurehead; someone wanting to do a biography . . . He couldn't be bothered to wade through all the kipple to find the updates.

"Anyway," Rackham went on, "you don't own Venus. No one does."

"Tell her to keep away from me," Singer said. Patiently waiting, he watched her and the ordinary Californian day beyond. A green fountain that reared into the unnaturally blue sky: an avocado tree. Spiralling lines of silver water droplets flung across the lush lawn by a sprinkler. A plane that drew its contrail (violet line dragged through seething red cloud: raped) from left to right, like an artist's signature, before Rackham replied.

"You tell her, Singer. I'm your mission controller, not your psychiatrist. Pull yourself together, you'll be on coast-to-coast news in a day or so."

"Twenty-eight hours, fourteen minutes."

She smiled. "Well, you're on top of *that*, anyway. How are you feeling, Lucian?"

"Nervous as hell."

"Look on it as the first step of your journey back."

"I can never return to Earth, you know that. My heart would give out."

The pause was longer than necessary for transmission. Eventually, Rackham said, "It's true you'll have to undergo . . . quarantine at Armstrong Station, but you'll get full medical coverage."

Singer had commissioned his own medical profile, knew well enough that the calcium leached from his bones, his enlarged heart and weakened arteries, the dozens of different effects on his muscles, couldn't all be reversed. He had been too long in zero gee, hadn't exercised as he should have. After rescue he could look forward to being, first, a medical curiosity, and second, a cripple.

He said, "Look, I have work to do, okay?" and switched off the transmitter. He heated a meal and took it to a port, raised the blind and squinted out at Venus while he ate. He was over the nightside now, nothing visible but occasional scratching of lightning against the ashen light. But he watched for a long time before he went to his cubby and took a sleeping pill, sealed himself into his cocoon.

He always needed medication to sleep, and despite his years in zero gravity his dreams were still filled with the sensation of flight or falling. He dreamed of the accident which had killed both his crewmates, but this time he was in the command module, alone, feeling the thrust tremble as the main engine malf'd, the ship tumbling uncontrollably, a routine mission to dump mapping satellites turned into nightmare. It had taken a week for the orbit to decay, and Singer, in the science and lifesystem package, had been unable to do anything to help. He dreamed now that he was falling through smog-coloured clouds, pressure closing on him like a great hand, acid and heat searing his lungs, and woke up shivering, a halo of sweat around his splayed dreadlocks, unable to remember anything of the dream but its terror. It was the day the rescue mission made its rendezvous with his station. It was time to start work again.

The crushed disc of the sun hung where it always hung; as always, whips of lightning flicked ceaselessly in the industrial light. Singer could hear their static across the broadband, a constant scratching pulse as if the planet were trying to speak to him. He activated all his systems and the surveyor rolled forward, treads crushing the little colonies of crystals which had sprung up around it. And stopped.

A long series of numbers had been scratched into the cliff.

Although they were already eroding in the hot, acid atmosphere, they were still legible, and Singer recognized at once what they were: a loran grid reference. He called it up, saw that it was only a few kilometres down slope, at the edge of the small, recently-extinct caldera. Let her stay there, he thought, but after he started work, chipping out fossils and holographing them and spitting them out, the thought nagged at him. As if she were broadcasting a low level signal, an itch in the analogue of his mind.

He backed away, shovelled loose rock into the intake where the components for the protective coating would be extracted. And thought, why not? Why not see her? Make it clear that she was to stay away from him. Strike a bargain, down here where they couldn't be overheard.

The valley widened to a vast boulder field that, although it actually sloped down, always seemed to rise all around because of the refraction, as if he were a ball-bearing in a cup. Here and there clusters of crystal glinted: blood garnets, dirty rubies, amongst the rubble. Some of the boulders were bigger than the surveyor; a few were as large as the station where his untenanted body lay. As he rounded one of these he saw the intruder no more than a couple of hundred metres away, her outline softened by rippling waves of heat.

He called out on the broadband and she responded at once, a tickling voice that seemed to speak from his centre.

"Colonel Singer, I presume!"

"Dr McCullough."

"Dianne, please. Isn't this an incredible place?" Her effusiveness surprised him.

Her surveyor was a little bigger than his, its snout bristling with attachments, the drill-probe at its tail sunk in the ground. A beetle, he thought, an ovipositing beetle. And he a slightly smaller member of the same species, a tentative suitor. If she was at all unused to the climate of hell, she showed no sign.

"I'm just finishing a core for some UCLA geologists," she said. "A chore, I should say, but I have to pay some price to be here. This is such a—well, of course, you know all that. Listen, I wasn't going to visit you, but once I was down it seemed the right thing to do. I hope it was. It must be strange to have someone down here. After so long."

"Strange, yes." He was scornful of her enthusiasm, but also afraid of it. When he'd spoken to her before, while the rescue mission was still a million kilometres out, she had struck him as cold, remote, indifferent. Brain-in-a-box. But she was no longer there, trapped. She was *here*.

She said, "I think that what they want to do is a damn shame. I don't ever want to leave. There's so much to explore: a whole world. I thought that over and over on the trip out. I'm only just beginning to realize what it means."

"Most of it is flat, stony desert," he said. "This area is atypical."

She raised her drill probe and began to feed the core into a slot in her glistening body with a smooth, almost lascivious motion. "It seems to me . . . everything is strange, every boulder. I could spend the rest of my life examining the boulders, it seems." Her laugh was like a raster of static. "I'm sorry, I'm running away with excitement. But after all this time, the freedom . . . Not being told what to do. Not being monitored all the time. Solitude. It's bliss."

"Listen, Dianne, I came to say that I would be happy for you to stay away from the area I'm working. At least allow me that."

"Why are you still studying those fossils? I read some of your work. You seem, well, obsessed."

"I do? You don't think they're important? For one thing, they prove how common life may be."

"But they are all gone now; billions of years ago, when the sun finished its development and the greenhouse effect ran away, the oceans evaporated and everything died here. It's all history, they can't come back. You look at those and not the crystals?"

"The crystals are not alive."

"Some people say they are. They grow and reproduce."

"They are simply a product of the special conditions here. Or has there been new work I don't know about?"

"All those arguments confuse me. They seem alive to me."

"Come on," he said, openly mocking.

"I can feel it. In the crater to the east there are millions of them. You can hear them singing."

"Millions? There were only a few when I surveyed this place."

"I'll show you," she said and neatly swivelled, turning within her length. Singer followed, his tracks printing lines parallel to the tracks Dianne McCullough left on the baked ground. As they travelled, she kept up a ceaseless chatter, but Singer, uneasily feeling the first prickling of betrayal, said very little. They were replacing him with this untried, untested woman? She wasn't even a scientist: before her accident, she said, she had been a diving engineer. True, she handled the surveyor well enough. He admitted this grudgingly, knowing that already she was as adept as he. As if the low-slung machine were her natural body instead of a tool. Once, she ran it in a little dance while she was waiting for him to catch up, waving probes and extensors in exultation while lightning crackled through the murk above.

"I can hear them already," she said, "can't you?"

He went along with the game and asked for the frequency; but even at maximum amplitude he caught only a faint chirring that could have been static from some storm on the other side of the planet, botched by discharges of nearer lightning. Ahead he could see the rim of the caldera. Although only recently extinct, its lavid sides had already eroded to a broad flat-topped bank that seemed to warp upwards to the right and left.

"Oh be careful, please be careful," Dianne McCullough said. "You're running right through them."

There were not many at first: unfaceted, not really crystal-line, more like melted lumps of quartz. But when they gained the top of the bank he saw that the slopes of the caldera were covered with them, newly grown singletons glittering amongst pebbly accretions of older formations, low spires and twisted towers stretching away into the sullen distances.

"I haven't been here for two years," he said. "There must have been a change in the wind pattern, bringing precipitate in from the active volcanoes." He gestured southwards with several limbs, at the point where, at the fading edge of visibility, tipped sideways by refraction, low distorted cones sat amongst whorled lava fields.

"When I was resting," she said, "some formed around me, small ones no bigger than my thumbnail. When I had a thumbnail."

"It's the protective coating. They seed in it like paramecia in a hay infusion."

"I think they're singing some incredibly complicated song. Did you ever hear whales singing? The same song, the same story, lasts for hours."

But the chirring was as faint as ever. All around, hell simmered.

"I never want to leave," she said.

"The surveyor won't last more than a dozen years."

"They'll be sending me another one at the next window, and perhaps a remote to explore the upper atmosphere. There's so much to explore."

"You're staying here? The expedition is staying here?"

"They'll leave all that remains of me in orbit. But I'm not going back to it. You made the first step; I'm going a little way beyond."

"Damn Rackham!" Angrily, he began to disconnect even as Dianne McCullough began to speak again. Her voice faded and he swam through an instant of blackness to his feeble body, felt it shudder on the couch. But when he opened his eyes he saw a shadow eclipsing the constellations of telltales, a man regarding him steadfastly.

"Hold still, Singer," the intruder said. It was Buddy Sarowitz, commander of the rescue mission. "Hold still now. Man, how did you ever get to looking so bad?"

*

The next few hours passed in an uncomfortable mêlée, confusing and exhausting Singer. He felt himself at a remove from both his rescuers, even as they spent two hours cutting away his tangled dreadlocks and washing the remaining hair, trimming his beard, preparing him for the staged confrontation that would go out across the networks, the handshakes across the tunnel which joined Singer's station to their ship, the smiles and backslapping, even cigars, which left a raw taste in Singer's mouth and which were doused as soon as the cameras were switched off and mission control had given its opinion that it had been a great show.

Afterwards, the two intruders were reservedly polite towards Singer, neither quite sure what to make of him. Bobby Sarowitz shook his head over the variety of gimcrack techniques Singer used to keep the station running, while the science specialist, a young man named Lawrence Donnell whose skin was several degrees blacker than Singer's, seemed a little in awe: as if Singer were some relic from the past, a combination of John Glenn, Chuck Yeager and Neil Armstrong. Both annoyed Singer, Sarowitz's professional cynicism, Donnell's respectful sidelong glances. But what annoyed him most was the continual presence of their meaty, clumsy bodies: both assiduously exercised in a centrifugal segment of their ship at the beginning and end of each working day. They would not be cripples when they returned.

Singer stayed in the station, in his own territory, and after a while the others began to leave him alone. Almost the first thing Sarowitz had done was pull the control key of the link, and he wouldn't return it, no matter how much Singer argued that he had to finish his research, that he could be of help to McCullough. He complained to Rackham about this further betrayal, but she simply said, "That's the way things have to be, Lucian. You've got to accept that you're coming back."

"You're treating me like some sort of addict, making me do cold turkey."

"Just cooperate with Sarowitz and Donnell. They have a lot of work to fit in before departure. Why can't you help them?"

"The best thing I can do is keep out of their way, which is what I'm doing." It occurred to Singer that the plug had been pulled in case he decided to stay, take refuge on the surface in the surveyor until the rescue mission had to leave. He said, "I'm not going to pull any stunts. I'm no cyborg. I have to keep coming back or I'd lose memory when I was retranscribed."

"I'm sorry, Lucian. I have my orders."

And so did Sarowitz and Donnell. No amount of sweet-talking could convince them of the necessity of using the link. As his initial politeness faded, Sarowitz barely hid his contempt at Singer's plight. He could understand the rebellion – most astronauts are in a continual state of ferment against the armchair fliers of mission control – but he was of the old school, had come up through the Navy, and believed that you make your own luck. And besides, he despised the way Singer had let his body go. Donnell was more sympathetic, but he had his own problems.

"She hardly talks to me any more, keeps going off on Mickey Mouse trips of her own."

"She's enjoying herself down there." Singer tried to imagine what it would be like to be let out of the bottle. After the elective surgery, all that had been left of her crippled body was her brain and a coil of spinal cord, a few glands, her heart and a pared-down blood-system. Everything else, all that made her human, had been flensed away. Her blood was a synthetic compound oxygenated by a cascade filter; a dialyser swept out the wastes and balanced her electrolytes, her nerves were connected to computer interfaces.

"She keeps going on about the crystals, like an *idée fixe*, you know. An obsession. Mission control reckons that she's still within parameters, and she does all the scheduled tasks, but she won't talk, hardly."

"So when she comes up here, hold her a while. Like you're holding me."

"Hell, she doesn't have to come up." Donnell tugged at his neat, pointed beard. "That's the way it's designed."

Singer pressed for an explanation, and Donnell told him that

Dianne McCullough's incoming memory was skimmed each day and transmitted to the cyborg, read into the chemical balances of the cells of her untenanted brain. "The problem is that it doesn't work from our end. She doesn't have to come up, and I can't make her."

"So let me go down, let me see what I can do. It sounds like she needs a touch of reality, that's all."

Donnell shrugged, the gesture turning him slightly. "It would be neat, but I just can't do it. Stay with it, Singer. You'll be getting a hero's welcome back on Earth. There's all kinds of interest in you again."

Singer knew: his files were jammed with appeals from networks for interviews, all of which he'd ignored. He said, "On Earth I'll be lucky to get about in a wheelchair, if I survive the trip down. No, I'll be stuck on Armstrong."

"Maybe they can do for you what they did for McCullough."

"I'm an operator. I've no desire to be a machine for the rest of my life."

"Yeah. She told me, you know, that I was redundant, that she was the next stage in evolution. One thing you could do is maybe talk to her from here. You've been down there so maybe she'll talk back. You'd be an anchor. You don't have to go down to give her a touch of reality."

"It's real down there too," Singer said softly. He was ambivalent about the idea, and even after Donnell had obtained clearance he put off calling McCullough for a couple of days. It was a link with the harsh landscape of his love, true . . . and it would also remind him of what he had lost. But in the end, desire won out.

"I'm glad to hear you again," Dianne McCullough's voice said. It was botched by rasters of static, seemed light years away. In the communication shack of his station, Singer closed his eyes and imagined the simmering, sullen desert, ached for it. He asked how things were.

"Good. I'm still around the crater."

"You still believe those crystals are worth looking at? It's all been done before."

"The chemistry isn't everything."

"What else have you found?"

"Did you ever notice the way they all interconnect? I can almost understand it. But not quite, not yet."

"I wish I could be there."

"I don't mind being alone. Would you ever leave your body for good?"

"No, I don't think so."

"That's the difference between us," she said, and cut contact.

Still, Singer was more successful at drawing her out than Donnell, or so Donnell said. He had other conversations with her, and always she was vague and distracted and abrupt, so different from when he had talked with her on the surface. He found that he drew her out most by talking about the crystals. She had the idea that they were linked all the way around the planet, that they might even keep the atmosphere the way it was, so that they grew in optimal conditions.

He laughed. "That's teleology. If the atmosphere wasn't the way it was, they wouldn't be there anyway. They need heat and acidic conditions and great pressure, lots of electrical activity, free fluorine and so on. Without any one of those, they wouldn't be there."

Laughing at her ideas was a mistake: she withdrew, cut contact. Another time he asked, "Do you miss people?"

"I always was a loner, you know. That was partly why I became a diver. Used to spend months at a time tending the mining machines. Under pressure like here, but darker of course, and so much colder." She had worked in the Pacific mines, until one day she had come up too quickly and a nitrogen bubble had formed in the artery supplying her spinal cord. After that she had been a tetraplegic, until she volunteered for the cyborg programme.

She asked how he took to having company again. "Those two annoyed me, you know. They don't know they're redundant, meat machines."

"I guess I'm one too."

Her laughter was unnerving, like fingernails scratching tin. "You're an amphibian, Singer, a lungfish. I can tolerate you."

She meant it; she wasn't talking to Donnell at all, now, and was falling further and further behind with her scheduled tasks. Even Sarowitz was becoming worried; the Jupiter mission he and Singer had once trained for had been revived, and he had a chance at it if this one went well. More than once, Singer tried to use Dianne McCullough's non-cooperation as a lever for getting back down, but to no avail.

"Christ, Singer, you know I can't let you." Donnell pulled at his beard. "Orders, right?"

"Well, of course." Singer knew with heavy certainty that he was barred forever, and thought of his surveyor, its autonomic programmes running down, its casing eroding . . . The next time he talked to Dianne he asked about his machine.

"It's okay," she said after a pause.

"The maintenance programmes are running, then."

"I suppose so," she said, and changed the subject.

And so it went, until the flare.

Singer was working on a blocked pipe in the garden. It wasn't necessary now, but he kept the station's systems going out of pride. Cobbled together from the lifesystem and science package of the original mission, and half a dozen resupply canisters sent to him after the disaster, it was *his* place – some of the access tunnels were too narrow for Sarowitz and Donnell to manoeuvre their bulky bodies, and there was little of the neat order, defining spurious directions of up and down, shown in their ship.

He had just wrested a filthy clot of *Spirella* from the pipe when the signal bell rang. He ignored it, carefully vacuumed floating globules of alga-tinted water, refitted the pipe. He was fastening the last seal when Sarowitz caromed into the long, sunlit space.

He said, "There's a flare on the way. You better come to the shelter."

"You know, I've already received enough radiation in the

normal course of things to make me sterile." Singer carefully tightened the seal, switched on the pump. The tube shuddered under his hand as green water pulsed through.

"For Christ's sake," Sarowitz said, "we're already getting the first particles. Donnell is buttoned up. Now come on." He grabbed Singer's arm, his fingers meeting his thumb around the wasted biceps.

Glaring, Singer shook off the grip. "I'm not an invalid. Not here."

"Then come on," Sarowitz said, embarrassed, and turned to go.

After a moment, Singer followed him.

They spent two weeks in the cramped shelter while the radiation of the flare sleeted through the rescue ship and Singer's station. It was only a minor flare, would hardly disturb radio communications on Earth – although it knocked out spacecraft communications, which were not shielded by the magnetosphere and atmosphere – but to be out in it for more than a couple of hours would be to receive a lethal dose. Donnell, fretting about the science programme, said that he was beginning to think that Dianne McCullough was right, space was a place for machines, not people.

Sarowitz sneered. "Survival is an engineering problem. They've developed new shields for the Jupiter mission, and when they're fitted to all spacecraft we won't have to sit in a lead coffin whenever the sun hiccoughs."

"He has a point, though," Singer said.

"You're falling in love with that cyborg, man," Sarowitz said, good-humouredly.

"Come on," Singer said, uncomfortably. And wondered what she was doing at that moment.

In the meantime, he found that Donnell played a passable game of chess, and they held tournament after tournament while Sarowitz watched the old flat films for which he had a passion ("That Kathleen Turner, man. She's all I need on a mission like this!") or read technical manuals, reviewing his tensor calculus. Two weeks. And when the storm finally died there were only five days until the mission was due to depart.

Once it was safe to leave the shelter, the first thing that Donnell did was activate the radio-link with the surveyor. Singer hung at his shoulder while Donnell fine-tuned, flipped to another channel and tried over. At last he flipped off the power in exasperation and silently began to pluck off the access plates and check the circuits. Singer watched with a kind of numb anticipation, knowing that there would be nothing wrong with the radio.

There wasn't.

Sarowitz, hung upsidedown in the hatch, said, "Want I should suit up and check the antennae? They could have been fritzed by the flare."

Donnell turned from the link panel. "There'll be no need," he said quietly. "She turned off the update link a couple of days after the flare began; I guess that's when she turned the radio off too."

"Christ," Singer said. Without the link, Dianne's uninhabited brain would receive no memory updating, and she'd been down there too long now; if she returned she would lose memory in patches, holes.

This had to be explained to Sarowitz, who simply said, "I still think I should check the antennae." And suited up, went out, came back two hours later, shrugging wearily. There was nothing wrong with the antennae.

"You'll have to let me go down," Singer said. "That's the only way we can find out what she's doing."

"And risk losing you?" Sarowitz asked bluntly.

"Come on," Donnell said, "Lucian has a point." Behind him, green water pulsed through tubes as thick as his waist; they had gathered in the garden of Singer's station, the largest open space in the conglomerate structure. Blades of sunlight lanced through the air from between the shutters of the curving, half-closed blinds.

Sarowitz glanced back through the hatch, where he hung, arms folded, toes of one bare foot holding him in place, swaying in air currents like a huge bat. His glance took in the red-lit couch and console of Singer's downlink, partly visible beyond the communications shack. Clearly, he was wondering if Singer was going to pull some trick.

So Singer said, "I'm coming back. I'm not like McCullough. I couldn't live in a machine."

"Suppose there's something down there, something about those crystals she was always babbling on about." Sarowitz glared at Singer, at Donnell.

Donnell said, "When you're down, I'll load a parasitic program into your dump memory. If you get that into the system of *her* surveyor, it'll activate the retrieval system. We'll get her back, even if she is partially amnesiac."

"Hell," Sarowitz said, "can't you load that into her from here?"

Donnell shrugged, caught at a handhold to steady himself. As always, Singer watched these clumsy twitches of overdeveloped muscles with distaste. He hung quietly in mid-air, warm sunlight splashing one hip.

"Well?" Sarowitz demanded.

"I can't broadcast it without knowing precisely where she is. Too much atmospheric interference to do it otherwise, she'd only get part of it. Singer can push it right into her."

"Call up Rackham," Singer suggested.

"Hell no," Sarowitz said. "We can deal with this ourselves."

Singer tried not to smile. He had guessed that Sarowitz would not defer to higher authority. It would go against the code, it would rupture his cool. You didn't look for help to get your ass out of the crack – you did it yourself, or died trying.

Donnell pointed out, "We don't have much choice, Bobby. Either wait for Dianne to call in, until it's too late to do anything, or send Lucian down."

"Don't push so hard," Sarowitz said, scowling. But he speared two fingers into the breast pocket of his coveralls, fished out the master key to Singer's link. He flicked it down the length of the garden, a tiny precious fish flashing silver through spaced blades of sunlight. As Singer plucked it out of the air, he added, "And don't you mess up."

"Come on," Singer said, grinning. "I *know* Venus."

The stretching moment of blackness . . . then sweet rushing fulfilment. Immediately, Singer began to scan the distorted landscape, and realized with a shock that the surveyor was nowhere near where he had so precipitately abandoned it, at the edge of the caldera. He checked the loran grid, found that he was some five kilometres south. How had he – or rather, the surveyor – ended up there? Left to itself, the machine possessed only the skimpiest maintenance functions, little more than shovelling up rock, available anywhere, and processing it into the protective coating of fluoro-silicones.

He swivelled again, failing to see Dianne's machine. Crystals shattered under his tracks. They were on the surveyor as well, clustering thickly around the antennae, and he reached back with a fine manipulator, brushed them off. Perhaps the surveyor had moved away from the thickly seeded caldera simply to prevent itself from being overgrown, he thought, and felt relief at being able to rationalize the mystery.

He called up the station, and Donnell answered, fed the programme to him. "How is it down there? Any sign of her?"

"Not yet. Switch off, now. She may spook if she finds I'm in contact."

"Okay," Donnell said reluctantly, and Singer was alone. Or, not quite. As he moved off, scanning radio frequencies and failing to raise Dianne on any of them, he felt a faint cold touch, an alien presence within the circuits where his mind nestled, a ghost in the machine.

But he shook off the feeling as he travelled, revelling in the power of the surveyor, his body, as it rolled across the ground, shards collapsing crisply under his treads as lightning scratched and scratched in the murk above, his twenty senses registering everything around him in the furnace light.

He'd taken speed a few times when he was a teenager, and being the machine was like that high: every sense sharp yet his limbs lightly sheathed, swaddled. Exultant, Singer rolled on, eagerly scanning all around him for any trace of Dianne Lee McCullough.

He found her on radar ten minutes before he picked her up visually, a glittering speck on the seeming rise before him, the caldera gleaming beyond. All around, the ground was criss-crossed with fading tracks, each limned by lines and strings of tiny crystals. The surveyor stood at the centre of this mandala, a glistening armoured beetle bristling with drills and probes, spurs and spires of crystal around the antennae and sensory turret like surrealistic crowns.

"Dianne?"

There was no reply. He circled the surveyor, baffled. From the growth of the crystals he estimated that the newest tracks had been made at least five days ago; but the growths on her surveyor were at least twice as old. Still something nagged at his mind, a tickling residue. He scanned all the channels again, and on impulse settled on the one where she had demonstrated the chirring she had claimed to be the voice of the crystals. The chirring was still there. And, after a while, a faint call.

Singer?

"Dianne! Dianne, what's wrong?"

Abruptly, her surveyor jerked into life and began to back away, drill probe raised like a scorpion's sting. He followed slowly, but she put on speed, bumping up a slope of pitted lava. Behind her, the caldera was a tipped bowl carpeted with spines and spires and twisted outcrops of crystal: an Ernst painting viewed through a dark distorting glass.

"Singer. So you came back."

Her voice didn't seem to come through the radio, but vibrated within the circuits which contained his mind like an echo in the vault of his skull.

"Why did you cut contact? Is something broken?"

"I don't need the meat anymore."

"You sound very sure. What are you going to be instead, part of the landscape?" When she didn't reply, he said, "I mean the crystals growing on you." He was relaxed and confident, the parasitic program in his dump memory a shaft with which he could pierce her at any time, pin her down and send her back.

"The crystals help me see."

"See what, Dianne?"

"I'll show you," she said, "but it would have been easier if you hadn't knocked off the crystals on your antennae."

"I don't—"

"Wait," she said, and suddenly the faint alien presence became real, like a person standing just behind him. Some sort of override, he realized, even as its grip tightened. A mist seemed to thicken all around, clouding every sense. He floated in it without panic – for panic is a glandular reaction, and his mind was cut free of his glands: cut free, it seemed, of everything – but with increasing fear. What had she done to him? Where was she?

"Over here," Dianne Lee McCullough said, and her voice candled a white vision of a woman sitting on a rock. For a moment Singer thought that he saw fairy wings glistening on her back. "My joke," she said, and vanished like a pricked soap bubble. "I'm sorry, this is too difficult to maintain. You really shouldn't have knocked off those crystals. They help the link."

"You put some program into my machine, didn't you? Was it you who moved it?"

He saw a great flat plain now, stretching under a darkling sky dominated by a patchwork ball which he realized was the sun seen by radio-light. Sparkling loops and curves, the magnetic lines which channelled prominences, wove a delicate filigree around it. The rest of the sky was faintly white, the residual microwave radiation of the explosion which had begun creation, and stars hung against it like ragged blooms. Here and there, small and clear, were the curdled spirals of radio galaxies.

He said, "What are you trying to tell me, Dianne?"

"This is how the crystals see the universe. The crater is like the bowl of a radio telescope. With others it forms a baseline as big as the planet. Every node of crystals is part of a greater intelligence: call it Cytheria, if you like. This place is like a room in it; in one way it's a library, in another a consensus space."

Without form, a dimensionless viewpoint, Singer considered. Somehow she had cut free of reality, worked out this hallucination or fugue, had imprinted it on his machine. And then he thought of the crystals growing on her surveyor, and on his: why had they clustered around the antennae when every part of the machine was covered in fluoro-silicones?

She said, "Your machine began to move around after you left, once enough crystals had grown on it. They showed me how to get here."

"Can't they talk to me?"

"You're just a lungfish, Singer. You've gone as far as you can by yourself. You understand a little more than the meat machines, but only a little. I want you to learn, to think what we can do! I think that there may be other viewpoints living in Cytheria, astronauts sent out as radio-packages from other civilizations, sent the way your mind is sent into the Bronovski circuits, the way you become the surveyor."

He could feel the limits of the override now, like a subliminal image of printed circuitry beneath the glowing radio-sky. Searching for the point where it connected with his sensorium, he said, "Suppose you're wrong, Dianne? Suppose you've marooned yourself down here because of a delusion?"

She ignored this. "We've transcended the need for physical bodies. We don't have to rely on them, or on machines, to support our minds."

And then he had it. For a moment the circuitry gridded his vision, and then it all faded. Hell rose again in his senses, the warped bowl of the caldera, Dianne's surveyor facing his across the simmering murk.

She began to back away again. "You fought against it. How can I make you understand?"

"You wanted to share it, Dianne. That's only human." He couldn't say that it wasn't real. "It isn't a place for humans,

Dianne. It's too far out. Exploration means nothing unless you can return, unless you can share what you've found with other people. To be human is to, well, to need other humans."

"Ever since my accident, until the cyborg programme, I was stuck in a broken meat machine. Do you understand what that was like? Nothing but helplessness, dependency on other people or on machines, nothing felt towards me but pity. That's what being human meant to me."

He understood.

"That's what it will be like for you, if you go back. Here, you can be free."

"Until my surveyor breaks down."

"I told you that I've gone beyond the need for that," she said. "I can live in the consensus space." She was a very long way off now, distorted by rippling heat. When he made to follow, she wheeled around, moving away more quickly. "Don't follow. Go back, tell them that my machine broke down, that I'm dead. Go on, lungfish, back to the sea!"

She was still in range of his transmitter of course, but he didn't use the program against her. Not out of pity or sympathy, but because he knew that what she said was true. He watched until she was out of sight, then cut the link.

And after a moment was beyond the black instant of reconstitution, and lived again.

Donnell swam through the hatch and caught the edge of Singer's couch. "Did you find her? Is she still alive?"

Catching the other's hand, Singer shook his head.

It was not difficult to maintain the lie; after all, he was the only one who could disprove it. He went downlink several times more, to complete the scientific programs as best he could. Although he searched for it in the little free time that he had, he saw no sign of Dianne's surveyor, but sometimes felt an otherness, a presence in the furnace landscape. On his last trip he went to the edge of the eroded caldera and tried to hear the voice of the crystals, of Cytheria: but the faint chirring could have been anything or nothing. Still, he left the surveyor on the rim, where she could find it if she needed it.

During the long slow swing back to Earth Singer began to exercise in the centrifuge. Donnell tested him after each session to make sure he wasn't overdoing it, and after Singer had finally managed to run three times around the centrifuge torus at half a gee, asked him if he thought he would ever be fit enough to return to Earth.

"No, of course not. According to my medical profile things have gone too far for that. But there will be a maximum acceleration of half a gee on the Jupiter mission, at insertion. I'll have to be able to withstand that."

"You think they'll let you go on that?"

"Sure." Singer was confident about that, at least. Alice Rackham had called *him* up a week ago, to complain about the mail which was deluging her office. "If you have to stir it up," she had said, "do it with NASA. I work here, is all." And when Singer had promised to try: "You had better, mister! I'm knee deep in it already!" Then she had softened. "Good luck anyway. We're all rooting for you here."

Singer explained to Donnell, "I'm a hero, aren't I? Public opinion is on my side, and you know that NASA listens to the public. Besides, I'm the most experienced downlink operator they have. How can they refuse?" He tapped the picture of Jupiter which Sarowitz had fixed to the wall of the commons. "Bobby doesn't know it, but he's already gotten his first crewmember."

And three years later he was there, ready to descend into the banded world-ocean and still thought about Dianne Lee McCullough and the debt he owed her. For owe her he did. In recoiling from her rejection of all that was human, he had been given the impetus which had, finally, brought him here despite his handicap. One day, he knew, he would have to return to Venus. Although she had said that she had transcended her body, transcended her humanity, he wasn't so sure: for, in the hour of her rejection, hadn't she asked him to go with her? No human action is absolute, is pure. Only by our flaws are we redeemed. And suppose, he thought, suppose she had been right, suppose the crystals were alive, formed some sort of *gestalt*, reached out across the universe as Dianne had reached out to him?

Yes, he would go back, stand at the edge of the unknown and call to her. And see if she would answer his siren song, and tell him all that she had learnt.

The Temporary King

I'll begin as all the old stories began, and tell you that once upon a time there was a great forest in the shadow of a mountain, and in a clearing of the forest stood a house built all of logs, and roofed with living grass. It was the home of the Lemue family and the head of the family was my father; I was his youngest child and only daughter. That was how things were before Gillain Florey arrived.

I remember him even after all this time as well as if he had just now left the room. For I was the first of our family to see him, and I was the cause of his downfall. It was spring then, all those years ago. In the mud and new reeds beside the creek frogs were calling hoarsely each to each; there was a scantling of green along the limbs of the dogwood and alder trees and the flowers of the magnolias were just about blown; and every still pool was mantled with a golden scum of pine-pollen, wrinkling in the wind like the blankets of uncertain sleepers. It isn't the same here, under the dome, where you notice the spring only by changes in the quality of the light, if you notice it at all. When I was a child the lengthening days and the warmer weather were only a part of it. It was like a great reawakening, a stirring; and I felt the same stirring too.

I was seventeen then, yes, the same age as you. That's why I'm telling you this now. Seventeen, and I felt as if I had done everything that could be done in the forest. I felt trapped, closed-in, by the worn familiarity of home, by the prospect of marriage. Oh, I suppose I loved Elise Shappard, but it had all been arranged by his father and mine. I loved Elise, but not in the way you'll love, freely, of your own choice. I felt that there had to be more, but I didn't know what. My family and the house and a small part of the forest were all I knew.

So that spring day, when my mother asked that someone go collect ivy sap – it makes a good red dye, and we boiled some of our wool in it – I went gladly, carrying a pot and a small sharp knife up through the fern clumps that were just beginning to show new green buds beneath the pines. And that was where I found the man.

He was stretched full out on a bank of ivy amongst the roots of a leaning pine, boots crossed one on the other, his trousers of some shiny dark stuff, the flaps of his leather vest open on his smooth naked chest. His face was as white as a woman's and his hair long and tangled, like black snakes around his head. I remember how I hardly dared breathe as I looked at him, as if he was a vision conjured by the finest, most delicate of spells. And then his eyes opened. I dropped my pot and my knife, and I ran.

I made a fair commotion when I reached the house, scattering hens and geese as I ran yelling through the compound. People looked out of doors and windows to see what was happening and I'd hardly had time to begin to gasp out what I'd seen, a man, a stranger, up in the forest, when someone cried out a warning and we all turned.

In the distance someone emerged from the shadows beneath the trees and strolled down the grass slope towards the house as if it was his own and he was returning to it. He briefly disappeared when he reached the haha; then he had scrambled up the other side and started to cross the bare fields.

One of my uncles called, "Don't worry, Clary, we'll see him off!" and someone else swung onto a horse and, brandishing a staff, galloped towards the stranger. Behind him the others whooped and yelled encouragement. He swept past and the stranger ducked the staff, raising his hand as the rider – it was my brother Rayne – checked his mount and turned. And then the horse stumbled, ploughing into the ground in a tangle of legs and reins, Rayne tumbling over its head. Someone screamed and someone else fired a shot which sprayed dirt a metre from the stranger's boots. Tall, white-faced, he turned to us and once more raised his hand.

The air turned white, white as the sun. It felt as if your eyeballs had all of a sudden turned inwards and there was nothing in your head but cold white fire. It was so sudden that I didn't even feel frightened, was simply puzzled that I was lying on the ground with someone's boots in front of my face.

It was the stranger.

I picked myself up; all around everyone else was picking themselves up too. The men shuffled uncertainly, all of their oafish bluster deflated by the magic. A dog barked a challenge and someone hushed it. We were all looking at the stranger, who was looking at me.

I felt a kind of laughter bubbling inside, a singing in my head, and I brushed at my dress and stepped up to him. I still don't know why I did it; perhaps I felt responsible.

He smiled and held out my knife, hilt first. "You dropped this, Seyoura. I'm afraid your little pot was broken, though." The pupils of his eyes were capped with silver; there was something funny about his knuckles.

I became frightened, snatched the knife and backed off into my mother's embrace. But the spell was broken. My father, pulling on his beard, cautiously approached the smiling stranger, then stuck out his hand, which the stranger looked at, then shook. The other men, all my uncles and brothers, began to crowd around, grinning, asking him how he had knocked us all down, how he could knock Rayne's horse over without touching it (leading the horse, which seemed none the worse, Rayne came limping up, ruefully shaking his head but grinning like the rest). My mother had once said that the games of the men always required that someone be hurt, so that they would seem more important than they were; and now it was all over with no more than a sprained ankle to show for it they were babbling in relief. The stranger was the calm centre of it all, smiling and shaking hands, telling them that his name was Gillain Florey, please call him Gil, that he came from another world.

I wanted to see more, but my mother pulled me towards the kitchen, scolding me and worrying about what might have happened in the same breath. All the rest of the day and all that evening the kitchen bustled as we prepared a formal meal. My father had declared Florey to be the honoured guest of the house.

"Which simply means extra work for us," my mother said, sitting as usual on one side of the great fireplace, her fat naked arms resting on the arms of her high-backed chair as she watched her daughters-in-law and their children cook and carve and clean.

My grandmother, shrunken and frail in her own chair on the other side of the fire, said that outsiders always brought trouble, and it was lambing time too, you couldn't expect the men to care about that now. I was carding wool in the corner by the door, pretending not to listen. I wanted to sit at the feast and hear all the stranger had to say, but of course I couldn't. I was only a girl. The only reports I had were the breathless exclamations of the women as they brought out empty plates and waited to take in the next course. One told my mother that the stranger claimed that his family had once lived in the countryside around, hundreds of years ago; another said that he had a little metal stick, and that was what had knocked us all down. "Fancy all this happening to us," she said, and scurried out with a platter of fruits as big as her head balanced on one shoulder.

"A three day wonder," my mother said, picking at her own food. "And what good will it do us? That little stick won't get the lambs born or the seed sown, for all the men gape and gawk at it."

"In my day," my grandmother said, "we didn't have any of this trickery, not even the glowing-tubes. Just lanterns and candles. Though I do like the light now. It doesn't jump about so."

"One thing's certain," my mother said, "he isn't here to sell to us, much less give anything away. Live off us a while and move on, I shouldn't wonder. I'll have a word about that."

But I wanted the stranger to stay; I wanted to gawk, just like the men. Later that evening my fiancé rode over and we sat at the edge of the fields. His dog lay a discreet distance away, her head on her crossed paws, as I told Elise all of what had happened.

Elise was scornful. "He's probably just some fake."

"How could he do what he did? You're just jealous because your family didn't find him." I felt that the stranger was mine in a way; as if I had charmed him awake and led him to the house. Yes, just like one of the old stories. By defending him I was defending myself. "If you ask my father I'm sure he'll let you meet him; then you'll see he's no fake. He's real, Elise."

"I don't know."

"You ask. It's all right, you'll be one of our family soon enough."

"It's not that. I just don't want to, Clary. This man'll be gone soon enough and nothing will have changed, you'll see." And he leaned over and gave me a quick peck on the cheek. I leaned against him, stroking the bumpy top of his head through his short crisp hair. He was a tall, lean, gawky boy, but handsome enough when he smiled, and gentle. I hadn't any choice in the matter – like all marriages then it was an arrangement, and in exchange for my hand my father would have certain rights of passage over the land of Elise's family – no choice, yes, it's true. But I felt lucky about Elise, cared enough for him not to press him about seeing the stranger.

So we sat side by side in the twilight, the lights of the house behind us, the dark forest rising beyond the flat bare fields. The first stars were out, and you could see a few of the swift sliding lights that Seyour Mendana had once told me were ships and whole cities forever falling across the sky. I leant against Elise, feeling the hard muscles in his arm, his comfortable warmth, and wondered about the stranger, wondered which light he had stepped down from and why, until it was time for Elise to go.

Even after Elise had politely bid my mother goodnight and had ridden off, and I was lying in my own room quite unable to sleep, my thoughts were of the stranger, his white face and the way he had handed me my knife, the way he had lain there on the ivy in the forest, all unawares. He was somewhere in the house. The thought was thrilling and alarming and I listened for some sign of his presence but heard nothing except the usual night noises. And later, at last, I slept.

And the next morning, as if I had somehow stepped into a story where wishes come true, the stranger, Gillain Florey, came looking for me in the kitchen. He explained to my mother that he needed a guide for the day. "Just a little trip into the forest, back along the river."

My mother held the long braid that fell over her right shoulder and said that it was not the sort of thing a girl did. Florey smiled and told her, "Now, I know she goes up there because that's where she found me. And I can look after her. You saw my defences, right?"

"It isn't exactly that," my mother said uncomfortably. I'd never seen her like that before: at bay in her own kitchen, her kingdom, as if she were no more than what she seemed, a fat woman twisting her braid in a fat white hand.

Florey's smile widened. His silver-capped eyes. His white white teeth. "You're worried about her honour! I can assure you, Seyoura, that nothing is further from my mind. No, I need a guide, that is all, and I wouldn't divert one of your menfolk from their work. You know the problem I've been set. Well. I'm going up to solve it, if I can."

My mother began to deny precisely the thing she *had* been worried about and Florey waved a hand negligently. "Please, you have not insulted me. No, not at all. Where is your daughter? Ah, *there*. Yes, come now . . ."

So I went with him, my heart bumping as we passed through the compound and crossed the fields, people gaping after us as if we were a parade. We followed the creek into the forest and once we were out of sight of the house Florey sighed and slowed his pace.

"I thought they might follow us. Well, that's all right."

"They wouldn't—I mean, you're a guest."

He smiled and I blushed. "I'm glad to hear it. I hardly slept at all last night. Even with this." He drew out, from a pocket inside a flap of his vest, a little tube.

"Is that what knocked us all down?"

"To be sure." He showed me the clear lens set in one end and in his hand it began to shine, growing so bright that I had to look away, blinking back tears and green afterimages.

"Brighter than a thousand suns. Well, not quite, but bright enough to cause disorientation with nanosecond pulses at the right frequency. The silver in my eyes protects me from that, you understand? The other end is a sonic caster. It'll put you to sleep, like that poor horse, but its range is limited. And that's all I have, which is why I didn't sleep much last night. But I'm a guest you say. Well."

"What are you doing here?"

"To see the fabled ruins of Earth, of course. Escaping from civilization, if you know what that is. I can't believe the way you all live here. You're not in the net? No? Not even receivers? Not even electricity?" Each time I shook my head his smile widened until at last it seemed as bright as his light-stick. He laughed. "Well! Just about perfect. And no one bothers you here?"

"Only Seyour Mendana. And sometimes a flying machine brings a doctor."

"Who is this Mendana?"

"He buys the furs the men trap in winter. You're really from another world?"

"What? Oh yes, yes. Try and name one I haven't come from. Well. Looks like the MCC really do keep you sealed off. About time my luck changed; perhaps I'll stay here after all. Come on, then, let's follow the river. Your father wants me to solve a problem. You really can't cross it further up?"

"It runs too quickly, and there's a gorge, up beyond our land and the Shappards'. The creek is the border between us, you see. Down here there's only one path we're allowed to use on the other side, and we have to pay for that."

"That's what your father said."

For a while we climbed beside the creek in silence. Florey was awkward as he scrambled over the smooth white boulders the spring snowmelts had year after year tumbled from the higher slopes, and soon he was puffing and panting. As he perched on one great boulder, catching his breath, I asked at random – there was so much I wanted to ask – "What's the MCC?"

He looked at me. "To be sure, the child doesn't know who owns her. The Marginal Culture Council: the MCC. They're what keeps you safe from the outside world, though to be truthful if it wasn't for San Francisco I suppose the whole area would be sealed off."

"San Francisco?"

"A port. A couple of hundred kays from here. You really don't know, do you?"

"I'd like to. I'd like—" I paused, but I couldn't hold it back. "I'd like to see what it's like, outside the forest. Except I'll be married soon enough and then I suppose I'll be too busy bringing up babies."

"To be sure," Florey said quietly. I don't think he understood me. He got up and we walked and scrambled higher. When we reached a smoother part of the way he had breath enough to ask about my family. "I guess I should know who I'm staying with."

"You really were going to leave?"

"Really. I thought your father was after my stuff, so that's why I asked you along this morning. A hostage in case of ambush, but there was no ambush. Really, you can go back down now."

"I'd like to go with you."

"Okay."

Now it was my turn to ask about him, and he explained that he was from a very rich family who grew something that made people immortal, that his home was a castle on a world called Elysium. "People from this continent settled Elysium before the war, hundreds of years ago. In fact, my ancestors came from this very region, which is why I went to San Francisco. My yacht is there now, waiting for me. Ever heard of the Californian Substantivists? No? Oh well, it was a long time ago. Anyway, I'm fabulously rich and have little to do, so that's why I'm here. An important person. You might contrive to mention to your father that if I'm harmed a scramble rescue team will be out here at once. So he shouldn't get any ideas about kidnapping me, okay?"

I nodded solemnly: I believed it all, would have believed him if he'd said that on his world men swam through the air like fish, and slept on clouds. It was only later that I wondered why, if he was able to call up help so quickly, he had been afraid of anything my father could do.

But then, walking beside him over a thick carpet of pine needles at the edge of an ever deeper channel which the creek had carved for itself, I was too happy to think.

The way grew steeper and at last we reached the series of waterfalls and deep pools before the gorge, and climbed beside them using the narrow paths deer had made. At the top, at the edge of the cliff, Florey looked into the gorge at white water which thrashed amongst rocks towards the glossy lip of the first waterfall, then pointed upstream and shouted above the roar of the water, "That's where I'll have the sheep cross!"

"But they always go through the Shappards' land. And besides, sheep can't fly, not on Earth."

"No need. Your father explained that he has to pay each year for passage to the fields or whatever higher up."

"The summer pasturage."

"Whatever. Well, your father asked if I could help; I think he hoped I'd stride into the midst of your neighbours and drop them left and right just as I had to drop all of you last night when the men tried to make fun of me. I have other ideas." He gestured grandly. "I will have a bridge built. There, where the gorge narrows."

I couldn't see what he meant, and his talk about suspension ropes and load-bearing only confused me more. "You'll see when it's done, and your sheep will cross above your neighbours' land. Better than frightening people, eh?" Then he looked away sharply. "Who's that over there?"

After a moment Elise stepped out from behind a tree, his dog following at his heels. Florey ordered him to us and he came reluctantly, apprehension in his look. His dog watched Florey with her yellow eyes, her teeth showing between her loose black lips. I think that if I hadn't been there Elise would have run: men and their pride.

"He's my betrothed," I said to Florey, and told Elise, "I don't see what business you have following us around. If my father knew he'd be mad."

"This is common land, up above the waterfalls, your father has no say here. Anyway, I was on my way to lay traps for banshee." Elise was looking at the ground between his feet. "When I saw you, I thought . . ."

"It's true," his dog said, her voice a low growl.

Florey lifted Elise's chin and said, "A handsome lad, Clary." Elise twisted away, scowling. "You're lucky to be in line for such a fine, caring husband. But why does everyone think the worst of me?"

"We're not used to strangers, I guess."

"I meant no harm," Elise said. "I just wanted to see—"

"I understand," Florey said. He was looking at Elise's face, at the spike-jawed traps hung at his belt, at his dog. "Are you walking back with us, young man?"

"I really have to set the traps." Elise looked at me. "I'll see you later, Clary. Goodbye."

"Don't hurry on my account," I called as he walked away, but he didn't look back. I was annoyed by his following us, as if my independence had been diminished, as if he had already married me, already taken possession.

"You'll make a fine handsome couple," Florey said, and put an arm over my shoulder. We walked like that all the way back: I was never so happy.

*

For three days things went just as Florey ordered them. It was as if he had supplanted my father's authority, yet no one seemed to notice or to mind. The men felled a tall pine so that it lay across the gorge and another was sawn into four and, using chocks and levers, the pieces were set at either end. Under Florey's instructions a complicated web of ropes was strung between the spine of the bridge and the pillars, and a plank floor was laid. The men began to grumble that sheep would never cross it, but Florey simply smiled and showed them how to build high sides that leaned against the rope webbing. "What they can't see can't hurt them, and they'll follow their leaders. Sheep are like men, yes?"

I contrived to be near him as much as possible, taking up his food and running errands and looking after the notched stick and the weighted twine he used to work out how the ropes should hang. No, never so happy then. He had us all under his spell, whether he was striding about and ordering the men in short bursts of energy, or sitting with his back against a pine trunk, amongst the feathery shoots, his eyes closed as I watched his white face.

And in the evenings, there were his stories.

Florey would hold forth to the whole family for hours, pausing only to drink from the mug of cider I kept topped up for him as he told us about the other worlds: the singing stones of Ruby; the oleaginous oceans that girdled Novaya Rosya, boiling in summer and frozen in waxen floes in winter; the great canyon where everyone had to live on Novaya Zyemla; the beautiful empty sea coasts of Serenity. He described them all so vividly that we might have been there ourselves, and told tales at once so fantastic yet so plausible that the very trees seemed to lean closer to listen. Then he would smile and stretch all his length like a cat and say that it was time to sleep, and we would all be left gaping at each other, slowly becoming aware of the creek's babble and the mosquito bites we had not heeded, the cold night air and the babies and animals bawling to be fed.

Even Elise stayed still all of one evening, but afterwards he said to me, "Those tales don't really matter, Clary." He held one of my hands tightly, as if he was afraid I might fly away to one of Florey's fabulous worlds. And I would have, if I could.

"Gil makes them sound real. Isn't that the same?"

"He's got you bewitched, all of you in this house. That's what my father says."

"Your father's just jealous. So are you."

He ran a hand over his head, his short hair making a crisp sound beneath his palm. "I guess I am. Aren't you to be my wife, Clary?"

"Oh yes, it's all arranged."

"Except that bridge means your father won't need the bride price anymore. Do you think he'll still let you marry me?"

It hadn't occurred to me that the bridge would make so much of a difference. "I suppose it's gone too far to be stopped." His anxious look touched me: I still cared for him, I realized. "Don't worry, I'm not going to run away from the marriage."

"Then you shouldn't be hanging around this stranger, like, like—"

"You aren't my husband yet, though. So don't tell me what to do."

We stood staring at each other, angry and frustrated. The frogs were croaking to each other down by the creek; in the other direction, by the house, someone sang a snatch of an old song, her voice clear and small in the night. *O the times they are a-changing* . . . Elise swore and turned on his heel and stumped off along the bank of the creek to where he had tethered his horse, beside the ford. His dog looked at me for a moment, then yawned and turned and loped after her master.

The next morning we hadn't been up by the bridge for an hour when Florey said suddenly, "Are there any ruins nearby, Clary?"

"Some. There are ruins everywhere, I guess. Do you want to see them?"

"Yes. Right now."

"But what about the bridge?"

Florey gestured at the men, naked to their waists, who were cutting and shaping planks for the sides. "They know more about carpentry than I do. I'll have to show them how to fit it all together, but that won't be until tomorrow at least. We won't be missed." He picked up the bag which contained the food I'd brought, looked at me with his silver-capped eyes, and smiled. "Don't tell me you're scared . . ."

For a long time we walked through the forest without speaking, Florey swinging the bag at the new, tightly-curled heads of ferns. Sunlight slanted between the dark layers of the trees; once we saw a parrot fly off, and a moment later heard its shrieking alarm call. But I couldn't stay silent for ever, and the question I most wanted to ask, because it was the thing I most feared, at last had to be spoken.

"Are you thinking of leaving?"

"Oh, I can't stay here forever." He grinned at me, then broke into a run. I ran too, chasing him through the clumps of fern underneath the trees, until at last we collapsed breathless with laughter beside the bole of an enormous pine, a grand-father of the forest.

For a while we did nothing but breathe hard, smiling at each other. Then Florey reached up to touch the trunk. "Look."

A glutinous tear of sap was oozing from a crevice in the papery bark. A scarlet beetle struggled in it. "Once upon a time your ancestors ruled over half this world, and half a dozen besides. Your ancestors, and mine. Now look at your people, ruled by Greater Brazil and not even knowing it, trapped in their little lives. Insects in amber. You're different though, aren't you?"

"I . . ."

"Sure. You want to escape." And he leaned forward and kissed me.

I pulled back, but only a little. His silver eyes were a centimetre from mine; his hands touched my face before he sat back, smiling.

His hands . . . I caught one, the left. The knuckles were

slightly swollen and I could feel something thin and hard sliding under the bump of bone in each.

"All right," he said, and made a fist. And from his knuckles sprang claws, black and curved to a point like thorns, the one above the thumb slightly larger, a spur like that of a bird of prey, tipped with translucent gold. "I had it done a few years ago, when I signed up and out. The freighter ended up on Serenity and this was the fashion there, briefly. Still comes in handy in fights, once in a while." He touched my cheek and I felt five pricking points, the nearest (the thumb) just beneath my eye. Now I did jerk back, and stand.

"I thought you had your own ship. You said . . ."

Florey brushed at his forehead. "Oh yeah, that." He stood too, brushing pine needles from his knees. "Can you keep a secret, Clary?"

"I guess."

"What I said when I first came here, about being rich and so on, that was to impress your father. So he wouldn't throw me out, so he'd take notice of me. Oh, I'm no Duke or anything, just a freespacer, but I do come from Elysium . . . and I'm not freeloading. That bridge will *work*. Understand?"

"A little." But I wasn't sure how I felt about him now, what his untruths meant.

"Come on, show me the ruins." He held out his hand and after a moment I took it. And like a fool led him on.

The ruins began as a long ribbon of clear ground between the trees; only thick spongy cushions of moss grew there. You walked along this and suddenly realized the rocks on either side were the remains of walls, all overgrown with grass and fern, and then you were in the middle of it, tall trees growing up through what had been houses, square doorways gaping like the mouths of caves. Some had left no trace but the shape of their cellars, deep pools of still green water over which clouds of mosquitoes swirled.

Florey poked around for a few minutes, then complained, "I

thought there'd be more than this. What happened to all the machinery?"

I didn't know what he meant.

"Metal," he said impatiently, "or plastic. Christ, it couldn't all have rotted away. There must be something worth taking. What's inside here?"

He stooped at a doorway curtained with ivy, and I caught his shoulder. "You can't go in there. Bears live in some of these old places. They can be dangerous."

"So can I." He drew out his light-stick and flicked it on, pushed through the ivy. After a moment I followed, my heart beating quickly and lightly. Holding his light high, Florey stood at the beginning of a spiral ramp that curved down and down. You couldn't see the end of it. Bright colours glistened on the walls in twisting abstract patterns. You felt that you would fall into them forever if you looked for too long. Here and there mud had been daubed in crude symbols: the traces of bears. I pointed them out.

"They live in the rooms underneath. No one knows how far it all extends. They say it underlies all of the mountain." I was cold in there, and I hugged my shoulders as I peered into the flickering shadows of the spiral ramp. "The bears can be dangerous. They speak a kind of American, but it isn't much like ours."

"Our ancestors, Christ. Why did they trouble to alter bears? They were crazy, Clary, you know? They did so much damage to the world at one time that they spent most of their energies afterwards putting it back together, changing animals to make them more intelligent, raising extinct species from dust. What do you think the bears are guarding down there?"

"It was all looted ages ago. Come on, Gil, please." I thought that I could hear something moving far below, in the darkness. After a moment he shrugged and turned to follow me out into the sunlight.

I sat in the shade of a little aspen that canted out from the remains of a wall and watched Florey prowl the ruins. The sunlight sank to my bones, and I closed my eyes. After a while

Florey sat beside me. His white chest, the single crease in his flat belly. His black hair tangled about his white face.

"Is it true," I asked, "about the people in the old days growing animals?"

"Surely. Plants too. Greater Brazil may have invented the phase graffle, but it's way behind the old biology. That was all lost in the war, like a lot of things. On Elysium, we lost Earth, you know."

"What's a phase graffle?"

"It keeps a ship together in contraspace. A sort of keel into reality, you understand? Otherwise the entropic gradient would spatter it all over the universe."

I sighed. "I wish I knew more."

"It's a big universe outside this forest. You're better off here, really you are." His silver eyes flashed in the sunlight. His knee leaned negligently against my thigh.

I don't know how it happened; the beginning was lost in the deed. But one of us must have made a move towards the other, a word, a touch. I don't remember whether it was Florey or me, but we were tangled together, kissing, and then he began to make love to me and I surrendered. It didn't last long. Afterwards I lay still while Florey rearranged his clothing and said, to the ruins, to the sky, "A virgin! Well, well. A virgin!" He seemed both delighted and amused.

A stone was digging into my shoulder and my skin stung where his claws had scratched all down my sides, but I lay in a kind of haze of fulfilment. I had changed something, made a move all my own, and as I tenderly watched Florey I imagined leaving the forest with him, rising amongst the lights in the sky with him . . . and then I remembered Elise. A kind of panic seized me and I began to cry, although there were no tears, just a sort of racking hiccough attack, absurd and not at all romantic. Of course Florey tried to comfort me and that made things worse.

"I won't tell," he said. "Don't worry."

"It's not that. It's . . ."

"Your fiancé, yeah. He kind of hates me, doesn't he?"

"He's just . . . just a jealous kid."

"Listen, Clary, I'm maybe ten years older than him, but that's all. I'm human too. I didn't ask to be raised into some kind of god. Jesus Christ."

"I think you could be head of my family, if you wanted."

"No, Clary, see, your father tolerates me because I'm helping him, raising his prestige. That's all. Listen, I'll have a talk with your young man, set him straight. He's kind of cute, you know. I'd be unhappy to think he dislikes me."

"I don't see how—"

But Florey smiled. "Don't I have a way with words, now? Come on, smile. That's it. I'll fix it up, you'll see. You ride a horse?"

"Not often."

"But you have, yes?" All at once he was brutally business-like. "So don't worry about your maidenhead, okay?"

I said helplessly, "I love you," and felt the guilty pang that goes with letting slip a lie, and didn't know why. Of course I know now that I was in love not with Florey but with the idea he represented, the idea of freedom, of flying away from the forest.

"You can't come with me, Clary. My life is kind of compli-cated right now."

"You've done something wrong, haven't you?"

He was silent for a moment. His silver eyes were unfathom-able, and I began to feel afraid. Then he sighed. "Yeah, you could say that. You won't tell anyone?"

"Oh, we both have our secrets to keep." Everything, the bright sunlight spinning amongst the new leaves of the aspen, the soft green ruins, the spring air, mocked me. I was a dark discordant blot in the centre of it all. When Florey held out his hand to help me up I ignored it, and we didn't touch, and hardly talked, all the way back.

At the house I went straight to my room and scrubbed the dried blood from my thighs and my dress with cold clean water, rinsing over and over until my skin was red and sore. Then I lay down and cried, real, hot tears, but not for long, and went down to the kitchen and helped prepare supper as if nothing had happened. If my mother noticed anything she kept it to herself.

That evening as usual Florey sat out near the creek with a half-circle of people before him as he recounted one of his stories. I could hear his lilting cadence from my bedroom window, all meaning botched by distance, and I had to pull my bolster over my head so I could sleep.

The next morning I didn't go up into the forest but worked in the kitchen preparing vegetables and then scrubbing the long scarred pine table until it shone white and my fingers were raw. It was a kind of penance. My mother watched me work, and at last brought me a parcel of food.

"You'll be carrying this up to your friend, I suppose."

I had to take it: to refuse would have been to admit that something had happened.

"Clary," my mother said, and brushed her long hair back from her round face, "child, I haven't said anything before, but be careful. He's a stranger, remember, not our own kind."

"Don't be stupid, mother."

"Don't you be, Clary, that's all. Think of Elise. You're hurting him, and by doing that you're hurting both families. Life has to go on, Clary."

"Oh, of course. Everything has to be as it always was." My grandmother was watching me, from her corner, her sunken eyes bright in her wrinkled face, and suddenly I felt trapped. I grabbed the parcel and ran out, was crossing the fields before I remembered that I didn't want to see Florey.

But he wasn't at the bridge; my father told me that the Seyour Florey had gone on up. "He said that he wanted to see what it was like. An odd one, eh, Clary?"

I remembered what Florey had said about seeing Elise, and felt cold. Things were getting out of control. I would have fled after him, but my father began to tell me about the work on the bridge. This was meant kindly enough; he thought that I was interested, didn't see my panicky impatience. "I don't know why we didn't think of it before, but it's a fine idea." He scratched his grizzled beard. "You're like me, aren't you, Clary? You like new things. Not like your mother, keeping herself in her kitchen." For it was my father's idea, not wholly inaccurate, that my mother was forever plotting against him.

My brother Rayne was chopping a pine log into wedges while my father talked: the sound of his axe rang amongst the trees and each blow was like a blow in my heart. At last I could bear it no longer.

"I have to go," I said, "so the Seyour gets his lunch."

"Oh, he'll be down with us soon enough. Wait up, Clary!"

But I was already halfway across the new bridge, the rough unseasoned planking swaying under my bare feet so that I had to cling to the rope hand-guide. The cladding was only finished on one side; on the other I could see, fifty metres below, thrashing white water. Droplets stung my face as I went, and then I was safe on the other side and I turned to wave to my father before I went on, climbing through the forest towards the high pastures.

I left the trees behind and fresh breezes blew down the grassy slopes into my face; beneath my feet the turf was as warm as fresh-baked bread. Our family's sheep should have been at pasture by then, but the men were waiting until the bridge was built, and their small, turf-roofed hogans were shuttered and empty. Higher up I could see the Shappards' flocks slowly moving against the green mountainside; higher still the snow-covered double peak flashed in the sunlight.

My worries seemed to fall away as I climbed, insignificant beneath the vast blue sky. I dissolved in the breathless now of the spring day, swinging the greasy parcel of food as I tramped upwards, stopping now and then to sprawl on the turf and look at the line of the forest below, the long, tree-clad ridges that saddled away on either side, vanishing into the hazy distances. Some day I would find out what was beyond them, even though I would be married to Elise. If my mother could handle my father, I could handle him.

And then I saw Elise's dog.

She came running towards me at her full speed, overshooting and turning back to posture frantically, so excited that her few words were no more than panting barks. "'ome, 'ome," she managed to say at last, "follow me, 'lary!"

I asked what was wrong, but all she would say was, "Ba'. Ba' thing. 'ome!" And she grabbed my wrist, pricking it all round with her teeth, tugging gently but impatiently.

Sheep scattered before us as I followed her, the bells of the leaders clonking dully. A high bluff jutted out of the slope, cloaked in blueberry bushes. When we reached it, the dog circled me, then growled, "Ba' thing," and led me through the bushes.

And there, in a hollow on the other side of the bushes, I saw them. Elise and Florey.

Both were naked, moving like starfish on each other.

And I ran, plunging through the bushes with the dog at my heels, outpacing her as she turned back to her master. I remember thinking that I mustn't drop the parcel of food, otherwise they would know who had been there. That seemed important at the time. If they didn't see me it would be all right. I didn't stop running until I reached the first trees, and then I had to stop, and leaned against the fragrant bark of a pine as I sobbingly caught my breath.

At last I could go on, and I took the old path down, my mind as empty as the shafts of sunlight that fell between the trees. The path followed a ridge around the valley in which the Shappards' house lay, its tangle of roofs and pinnacles small in the distance as a toy's, and I broke into a run again, crossing the ridge and plunging down through the trees, leaping from white stone to white stone at the ford and running on towards my own house. My mother was in the yard feeding the chickens – and then she saw me and dropped the little sack of grain just as I crashed into her oh-so-familiar bulk.

It all came out in bits and pieces. I would start to say something and then begin to cry, shaking my head away from

my mother's soothing hand. But my mother was calmly insist-
ent, listening to all I had to say but not believing any of it until
I timorously showed her the scratches Florey had made along
my flanks.

"Child, child."

My aunts were all there too, by now, watching me to see if I
would explode or change into a lizard, do something at once
wonderful and dreadful. But I did nothing except cry, quietly
and steadily now, sniffing and wiping my nose on the back of
my hand.

"Child, child."

"Something," my grandmother pronounced from her corner,
"something must be done. Or he'll bring ruin to us all."

"Stop crying, child," my mother told me. "We'll think of
something."

"How can we do anything against him?" It was my aunt
Genive, nervous as a squirrel. "I mean, with that stick of his
even the men couldn't—"

"Men, Jenny, know nothing useful," my mother said. "We'll
be more subtle. Go on now and get some ivy leaves. A double
handful will suffice."

Genive opened her mouth, then saw my mother's expression
and darted out of the kitchen.

"What – what are you going to do?"

"Wipe your nose, child. We'll befuddle this Seyour Florey,
that's what, and take him down a peg or two as he deserves.
Duke indeed. He won't stay around here when we've done."
She lifted out the flagon of cider cooling in a tub of water and
poured it into a pan on the stove. The sweet sharp smell of
apples filled the room as she stirred, and when Genive brought
in bunches of ivy my mother plucked the leaves and one by one
dropped them into the pan. In her corner, my grandmother
chuckled and nodded.

"The old ways, oh yes. He'll see."

"You taught me," my mother said. Every face was intent on
her as she stirred; we must have looked like a coven of witches.
Now the smell of apples was tinged with something earthy and

bitter. My mother lifted the pan from the stove and said, "We'll strain it when it's cool. Clary, tonight you'll pour the Seyour Florey's drink for him when he tells his lies, and make sure he has his fill."

I nodded, although I didn't understand.

"You'll see," my mother said, and rumpled my hair. "Now, tell me what you know of his weapons."

As Florey talked that evening, spinning out a tale about the jungles of Pandora and the old ruins hidden within them, I sat at his elbow and topped up his mug with the adulterated cider as my mother had ordered. Earlier, Florey had cornered me in the yard and told me that everything was all right with Elise, he would come down later on and make up with me.

I nodded, not trusting myself to speak.

"You're trembling. You're not frightened of me, now. After our time in the ruins?"

"A little."

He laughed and looked around – no one was about – and bent and printed a kiss on my lips that burned all evening. Later, when I came up to him as people were settling around the stump on which he sat, a king with his court at his feet, and poured his first mug of cider, he winked at me and whispered, "Don't worry, Clary," and drank off a draught. I looked away, ashamed at my betrayal but feeling at the same time a sick eagerness for it to be over: that image of Florey and Elise burned in my mind as Florey's kiss burned on my lips.

As ever, Florey gulped down several mugs of cider as he wove the spell of his tale, my family spread before him and the evening darkening beyond the various ridges of the house. My mother was in the front of the audience, flanked by my aunts like a queen amongst her attendants, a gnarled walking stick I recognized as my grandmother's lying like a sceptre in her lap. I couldn't stop looking at her.

"More cider," Florey said, and I quickly poured, spilling some. He drank and held out the mug again, said to no one in particular, "Best drug in all the worlds, alcohol, because it's the oldest. Though I've something in my pack that would make you feel as if you were in the very hands of your God." He drank again, then pushed the mug into my face, saying, "Drink too, girl, go on." I closed my eyes and sipped. Sweet, with the faintest bitter tang beneath. My mother had put in mead to disguise the taste of the ivy. Florey tilted the mug, but I closed my mouth so that the cider ran down my chin and spilled onto my dress.

"Flower of the forest this, girl. Where was I? Yes, the ruins, circled by bare ground that had been poisoned to keep out the jungle, the ruins in the sunlight. Picture it," he said, and briefly closed his eyes. "But you all know about ruins, yes? Ruins all over the Earth. They're all around you. You're living out your lives—" he belched—"your lives in the wreckage of the past. It's in your faces, I see it in your faces, Christ, and your eyes too, like holes in the past." Florey leaned forward, staring intently at his audience. I could see a dark rim of dilated pupil circling the silver caps in his eyes. "You're feeding on me, on my words. No more."

People began to whisper; I saw Rayne say something to my father, who nodded grimly. The spell had been broken.

Florey staggered to his feet. "No more, no more tonight." He swayed, and cider spilled from the mug. "No more. Head too thick. Fresh air and exercise. Clary—" Florey turned and reached inside his vest, and my mother swung at him with the stick, knocking aside his arm and sending him sprawling, striking him again as he tried to rise. Then all the women were upon him and I saw his hands amongst them, claws extended, slashing and slashing again, and somehow he was free, staggering back while Aunt Genive knelt over a puddle of blood, her own blood dripping from her torn face. My mother stood over her; Florey's light-stick was in her hand.

The men were all on their feet now, and my father started to say something but my mother silenced him with a look. "He raped Clary. This guest you brought under our roof. He'll die for it."

Florey held out his hands, glancing at the crowd behind my

mother, glancing at me. "You can't hurt me with that," he said.
"I have protection, remember?"

"But I can put you to sleep," my mother said. "I know how
to do it: my daughter told me."

"Ah, your daughter."

Then Florey sprang, but not at my mother. I was seized and
spun and found myself pulled tightly against him, his claws at
my throat. "You can't put us both to sleep. Give me my
weapon."

My mother shook her head. Some of the men were beginning
to edge out of the crowd, and Florey called to them. "If you
love this girl you won't go for your guns, or follow me either.
I'm walking backwards now. Don't follow. Come on, Clary."

His right arm crushed my right breast; his claws pricked my
throat. I moved backwards with him, stepping amongst the
seedlings in the newly turned field, then onto the rough grass
beyond. My mother stood still, my family gathered behind her.
Then Florey grabbed my wrist and yelled, "Run!" and dragged
me towards the trees. People shouted and a deadening tingle
started up my back; then we were in the darkness beneath the
pines, my feet flying of their own accord as I struggled to keep
up with Florey's long strides. His grip was a circle of pain on
my upper arm; when at last we stopped and he let go blood
started from four closely-spaced wounds.

Florey looked back through the dark trees. "Sonics only
work at close range," he said, "fortunately. I thought we were
almost done for, girl, but they aren't following. Not yet,
anyway. Come on."

"They might leave you alone if you let me go."

"I don't think so. You'll have to come with me after all.
Don't cry. You wanted adventure." He pulled me close,
stooping so that his eyes glittered a hand's breadth from mine.
His breath was sickly-sweet. "There was something in that
cider. My heart is pounding in my head."

"My mother—"

"Oh of course, your mother." He gripped my arm and we
half-walked, half-ran through the dark forest, he talked and

talked, his fear bleeding out in ravings and threats and sheer bluster that I hardly remember now. All of us in the forest were barbarians was the gist of it; we had betrayed our inheritance. "Elysium sank low enough when war cut us off from Earth, but not as low as you. Just two hundred klicks away, girl, ships lift for every world in the Federation, while here it's all superstition and darkness. Christ! First you tried to make me into some kind of god, and now this."

He gave me a little shake, glared at me and dragged me on. We were near the bridge now.

And then I saw someone coming towards us through the shadows. It was Elise. When his dog recognized Florey she growled, her ears flat. Florey whispered to me, "Keep quiet, girl. Or I'll mark you so no one'll want you."

Elise hailed us cheerfully enough, but he was obviously puzzled. Florey grinned. "We're just out for an evening stroll. Hoped we'd run into you. How are you, boy?"

"It's dangerous in the forest at night." Elise was looking at me; I tried to smile, failed, and looked away.

"Don't worry, boy. You know my weapons. Remember? Go on down and we'll follow in a bit. I want to see how the bridge is holding up. Clary's father was asking after you earlier, seems he wants a word with you about something."

"Is it all right, Clary?"

Florey was watching Elise now, and had let go of my arm. It was my last chance, and I took it. I said, "I saw you both, this afternoon."

For a moment, neither Florey nor Elise understood; then it struck them both. Florey slashed at me but Elise's dog reached him first, knocking him down and climbing his chest, growling. Florey's fist swept across her muzzle and the growl became a high-pitched whine which cut off as Florey slashed again. I backed away until I fell over something, a pile of pine wedges with an axe beside it. As Florey scrambled to his feet I threw the axe to Elise.

"Now, boy. Now, Elise . . ." Step by step Florey moved towards Elise, who slowly backed away, the axe raised at his shoulder. "Remember what you told me, what I told you this afternoon? You don't want her I know; I can give you everything you want. Come on now."

Elise's face was a white blur in the twilight; I couldn't see his expression. He had reached the edge of the gorge and glanced at the drop behind him before he said, "No."

"Then I'll go. That will be all right, yes?" That cloying voice, smooth and sticky as honey. "Just go, leave you be." He was almost on Elise now. I couldn't move. And Florey reached out, just as Elise brought the axe down.

The blow swung Florey round. He sank to his knees, clutching at his chest; darkness spilled his white fingers. Elise swung again. Without a sound Florey toppled over the edge.

After a moment Elise threw the axe after him, turned to me. "I love you," he said, and ran. I called after him as he plunged across the bridge, but he didn't look back. Soon he was lost amongst the trees on the other side.

There isn't much more to tell. Outsiders came looking for Florey a few weeks later; it seemed that he had killed someone important in San Francisco and had been on the run ever since. But we had buried his body – it had washed up by the ford – and told them nothing. My father had the bridge cut down: I think my mother made him do it. For a while I used to climb up to the clearing where it had been and sit alone and think, but then I became betrothed to someone else.

No, not your father. I'm not quite done.

Things had changed. Florey's stories had spread amongst the families, and month by month a few people left the forest for the larger world; in turn, this slow exodus brought the curious to us, off-world tourists in search of the more outré corners of Earth, illegal hunting parties, once an archaeological team that spent an entire summer digging over the ruins where Florey had taken me.

And Elise came back, just once. Two years after he'd run away. He'd become a freespacer, sailing the sea of space between the stars, had gained a swaggering bold manner and sought to impress us with wild tales of the wonders he'd seen.

But we were no longer in need of stories. The old days were dead, buried with Florey, our oh-so-temporary king. They won't come again. Soon after Elise left the Forest I left too, abandoning my family and the kindly, slow-witted man to whom I'd been betrothed, whom I'd never really loved. And came to the city, yes, and met your father. As for the rest, well, you know it as well as I.

Exiles

When Sepuldeva and Rayne arrived at the field to meet their partner, down from orbit at the end of his shift, there was a small but noisy demonstration blocking the gate. A ship from Earth had arrived two days before, the first to reach Novaya Zyemla since the revolutionary government had begun the embargo, and its presence had inflamed the already feverish supporters of the People's Islamic Nation Party. The Greater Brazilian embassy had been ransacked and daubed with slogans; there had been a rally at which effigies of members of the trade council of the Federation for Co-Prosperity had been burnt. And now this, fifty or sixty people chanting in front of the gate in the high fence which surrounded the field.

Rayne wanted to push on through. He said, "Just listen to those bastards. What do they think, it's our fault? Man, we're hurting worse than they ever will." He and Sepuldeva had drunk the last of their credit in celebration of Stefan's return, and he'd skinpopped something on the ride out, too. His pupils were pinpoints in his vivid blue eyes; the mix of drugs overlaid a fine tremor on his motor control. He jittered from foot to foot, squinting into Procyon's searing light. He said, "They got no right to be here."

Sepuldeva said, "The cops will be on their side. You want to spend a few years in jail?"

"We're *already* in fucking jail," Rayne said. His long black hair was brushed back from his forehead, done up in bead-strung braids. Crystal, ivory, copper, jasper, jet, they rattled and chimed about his face.

He and Sepuldeva were standing in the shadow of the port complex's overhang, near the oval runnel which pierced its green-glass wall. Inside the fence, port cops looked on calmly as the crowd chanted a single phrase over and over. Most of them were women, dressed from head to foot in black. Black light printed slogans in the air above their heads, lines running around and through gross caricatures of the President of the ReUnited Nations, of the Greater Brazilian ambassador to Novaya Zyemla, of half a dozen other declared enemies of the state that Sepuldeva didn't recognize. The holographic images bobbed and weaved in sympathy with their hand-held projectors. And a huge crescent and star floated high above everything else, vivid red in the morning glare.

The field stretched away beyond, bafflesquares and fluxbarriers like a vast flock of grey sails. The nose assembly of the ferry which had brought the maintenance crews down reared above them half a kilometre away. Only a handful of ships out there, and only one of those intersystem, the freighter which had broken the fifty-days-old embargo, its arrival sending colliding ripples of rumour through the stranded freespacer community.

Rayne said, "I don't know how much more of this shit I can take."

"Just think about the credit Stefan has earned."

Rayne said, "Every day, *believe* it. But, see, we'd let him take first turn of the trick, we'd have known to trust him without paying his keep."

Sepuldeva said, "Stefan's fine. We have to trust each other here."

Rayne pushed back beaded braids. "You're so fucking straight it's unbelievable."

"But I'm right."

"I guess. Those bastards there are getting to me. I'm damned glad I don't understand what they're shouting." It was the nearest Rayne could get to an apology.

"The owners need us," Sepuldeva said. "As long as we stay together we'll see it out." Truth was, the chanting was making him nervous too. The grosha beer he'd drunk half an hour ago was coming on now, a tingling expansion of his whole skin.

Everything seemed separate and clear and distant, moments
strung like Rayne's beads.

Rayne said, "And suppose the goddamn government clamps
down further."

"The embargo is the only way they can hurt the Federation.
But sooner or later they'll have to start mining orthidium again,
or they won't have an economy left."

Rayne had turned away from the crowd; now Sepuldeva
turned too. Two Guildsmen passed behind the green-glass
curtain wall, their uniformed figures flickering through distor-
tion as if deep underwater. "We were Guild we wouldn't have
these worries," Rayne said.

"For me it would be easier to go straight, We're freespacers,
we're in the life—"

"This goes on there won't be any life left," Rayne said.
"Damn, I've this bad feeling about Stefan. I mean, he's just
another Red, like everyone else on this rock."

"There are some differences between Novaya Rosya and
Novaya Zyemla. Religion, for instance."

"I don't know about *that*. He speaks the language, man, he
could just melt into the countryside with our goddamn credit."

The crowd was making more noise, and Rayne and Sepuldeva turned round. The high gates were opening.

Rayne said, "Come on, the cops have got to let us through.
Suppose Stefan's let out somewhere else? He'd be gone, we'd
never know it."

"Stefan wouldn't do—" but Rayne was already starting
across the apron. Sepuldeva followed him out of shadow into
heat and glare, caught up with him at the edge of the crowd.

Rayne shrugged off Sepuldeva's restraining hand. He'd put
on little round wire-framed shades, black holes in his white
face. "Come on man, they're just a bunch of fucking Red zarks,
worst they can do is kill us."

One or two demonstrators had turned around, a man in a
many-pocketed jacket that hung down to his knees, a couple of
women so wrapped in black cloth only their eyes showed.
Rayne shouted at them, "Fucking Reds, right?" and gave the

revolutionary Salute, fist clenched up by his shoulder. The man grinned, white teeth in a neat black beard. It occurred to Sepuldeva that no one in the crowd could have heard Rayne over the chanting, and anyway, probably none of them could speak Portuguese.

Next thing, Rayne was shouldering his way through the crowd. Sepuldeva made to follow and someone leaned in close, yelled something in his ear. It was the man in the baggy jacket, black hair bushed around a red bandanna with a slogan printed on it in a dashed and dotted encephalographic scrawl. The man yelled again, saying it was no problem, freespacers okay, pounded Sepuldeva on the back and melted back into the chanting crowd.

Rayne was trying to get past a couple of cops as the two dozen or so freespacers ambled through the gate, only a few looking at the people yelling slogans at them. Stefan was there, his grip slung high on his shoulder. As usual, he was bare-chested. The pleats of his red trousers flapped around his ankles (his feet were bare too) as he strode towards Sepuldeva, Rayne suddenly behind him. Sepuldeva had a flash of black-clad women screaming at him all the way back to the quarter, but the crowd let them go and turned back to the gate, which was closed again. Individual shouts merged again into the single chant.

Sepuldeva shouted over it. "Good shift?"

"Dull. As you said. Almost good to be back." The muscles under Stefan's stubbled jaw shifted: a small smile emerged. His face was grimy, clean white circles around his eyes.

Rayne came around to his other side. "Next time I go up I'm gonna get me a reaction pistol, man, see how they like it in their faces."

"That's your style," Stefan grunted, easing a thumb under the harness of his grip. He was a lot more typical of freespacers than either Rayne or Sepuldeva: born on a colony world, he'd been crewing orbital shuttles at fourteen, then had worked out of Jacob's Rock around Sirius for three years, mining orthidium before coming to do the same in the asteroids of the Trojan belt between Procyon and its white dwarf companion. Stefan was only twenty now, tall, blond, taciturn. Like most of the freespacers caught in the embargo, he and Rayne and Sepuldeva shared shifts of a single trick, maintaining mothballed mining tugs, the only kind of job they could get.

Rayne said, "Hey, at least I got a style."

"A buzz is what you've got."

"Well, we had us a little celebration for your homecoming. Drank ourselves out of money, which didn't take long."

Stefan said, "I got paid. You'll get your share."

As they walked towards the runnel, Sepuldeva said, "I wish you guys could get on better."

Rayne said, "You just want us all to be one big happy family, huh? I get on with anyone. They don't get on with me, it's their problem. And there ain't no problem you can't solve by getting out and moving on. That's the life, man. That's why I like it."

The runnel's arch received them. Bands of white plastic alternated with thick, bubbled glass. Sometimes there was movement behind the glass, dim, green, broken. You couldn't see what it was, only that it was there.

"Politics?" Stefan asked, after a while.

Sepuldeva said, "The natives aren't happy about the ship which arrived while you were upstairs."

"Saw it. Know who it brought?"

Sepuldeva and Rayne related the various rumours as they left the runnel and crossed the wide lawns, following the other freespacers. A car was already in the station, half a dozen armed cops watching as the freespacers trooped into it. Rayne gave them the Salute before the door closed.

The gleaming ziggurat of the port complex dwindled as the car followed its track past sealed warehouses, empty service pits, the low buildings and concrete apron of a heliport. Vast tracts of alfalfa spread beyond, grown for atmospheric conditioning and the plastic industries. Far off in the clear air was the high horizon of the northern cliffwall, a reddish line against the dark sky.

The car was small, made smaller by a couple of Guild officers sitting at one end, stiff in their high-collared uniforms, hair cropped to a millimetre of their scalps. The freespacers took the other end, leaving a wide neutral zone. Someone was passing a joint around, using a pintail servo as a clip. Rayne was doing one-handed pull-ups on a grabrail, swinging back and forth, looking at the Guild officers, looking away.

Sepuldeva and Stefan sat side by side at the edge of the noisy freespacers. After a while, Stefan said, "Fellow I worked with, systems, said the Guild is recruiting."

"They always did like a captive audience."

Stefan laughed. "The life and the Guild like me and Rayne. Cat and dog."

"Where did you hear that?"

"On Earth, when I passed through from Jacob's Rock to this so-called easy berth. Port by the ocean. I liked the ocean. Big, pure. Place called Galveston."

"Rayne comes from near there."

"Explains a lot."

"A small place."

Stefan smiled. "You understand, if you try."

Nettled, Sepuldeva said, "Perhaps I understand more than you think."

Stefan laughed again. The car rattlingly decelerated as it plunged into the slums that ringed the city's prickly heart.

The freespacers' quarter was a single square block of the Ring's inner edge, crossed by the mono line in one direction, a freight canal in the other. The boarding house, where they stopped to drop off Stefan's grip, was a minute's walk from the station; the nearest bar was around the corner, sandstone walls crumbling from rusting beams, leaning over its reflection in the canal's oily water.

Inside, freespacers sat at tables, stood three deep at the bar. Their noise was a physical thing in the low-ceilinged room. Stefan bought beer, and he and Sepuldeva and Rayne each drank a deep ceremonial draught.

"Now I am back," Stefan said.

Rayne said, "Just one time I'd like to get drunk 'stead of buzzed. Some of the guys were saying someone's making jack from fruit juice and sugar."

"I heard that too," Sepuldeva said. "I also heard some mechanic got thrown in jail and flogged for owning a still."

"Yeah? Well, I don't know about that. I do know this fungus beer just makes you see things funny, doesn't help you get out of it."

Stefan said, "You be out of it soon. Up and out after Sepuldeva here."

Someone came towards them through the crowd. Small, black, intense: Mia gave a big smile and said to Stefan, "Baby boy, you been away a long time."

"Only a week. Drink?"

"I've got one going somewhere."

Sepuldeva said, "I haven't seen you for a while, Mia."

"Oh, I was around some guys who thought they could get me some work. They couldn't." Mia shrugged, still smiling. Her hair was frizzed out around her narrow feline face. Tribal scars notched the corners of her high cheekbones.

Rayne said, "Only one kinda work I can think they'd want you for these days."

"Fuck you," Mia said.

"I wish."

"The thing is, is it okay if I come back a couple of days?"

Stefan nodded; Sepuldeva said, "Of course." Mia had been sleeping on their floor for most of the embargo. She was an intersystem pilot; there was no work for her at all.

Rayne said, "You know you're always welcome, baby."

"The guy you're looking for is over in that corner," Mia told him.

"Oh yeah? Stefan here buys more beer send it over, okay?"

Mia wrinkled her nose when Rayne had gone, said, "How can you *stand* that guy?" and began to tell Stefan the latest gossip, the rumours about the ship from Earth.

To one side of their couple, Sepuldeva sipped at his beer. He suddenly wanted to write about the morning, but his notebook

was back in the boarding house. He was thinking about
freespacers, about worlds, about the trap Novaya Zyemla had
become, his first day down, when he'd sat for hours on the flat
roof of his boarding house, watching the slow rise of Ahd's
swollen disc, the gas giant of which Novaya Zyemla was a
moon. He'd taken a trip up to the top of the northern cliffwall
and looked out across the deep rift valley which was the only
habitable part of the world; he'd rented a p-suit and walked a
little way on the ruddy frozen dust of the true surface.

Other freespacers? Their explorations were limited to finding
the tolerant bars, the cheap eating houses, where they were
content to gossip, talk over old incidents, the price of a room,
of beer. Rayne had been to eight of the ten worlds, yet his
outlook was still that of some small-time, small-town kid:
Stefan had said as much. Worlds: their variety had hardly
touched Rayne, had hardly touched most of the freespacers.
Movement was more important: that was why every freespacer
on Novaya Zyemla fretted inside the cage of embargo.

For Sepuldeva, it meant that the boundaries of the ghetto
which had always been there were now as real as the rimwalls.
And he wanted so much to be out of it, even if it meant
returning to orthidium mining, scouring an asteroid a metre at
a time with a jet of ionized caesium, exactly balancing the
reaction as loosened quark-stuff, the heart of catalfission bat-
teries, impacted on the rock during the cataclysmic ejection of
material when Procyon's companion had become a white dwarf,
leapt the gap to the mining tug's collector. Killingly precise
work, bearable only because it paid well. But Sepuldeva was
good at it: and now his unused craft swelled in his fingertips.

Stefan suddenly thrust his face into Sepuldeva's. "Let's go,"
he said, his urgency meshing with Sepuldeva's surprise. "Drink
up, guy. After the ship I need to breathe."

A bitter worm of grosha beer moving down his gullet,
Sepuldeva followed Stefan and Mia through the crowd into the
vertical light of noon. Some guy pissing into his reflection in
the canal looked around as they went past: it was Rayne.

Rayne latched onto Sepuldeva, pushing a plump silvery

drinking bag into his hands and insisting it was good stuff.
Sepuldeva sucked on the metal straw, got a slug of what tasted
like sugary acetone, lost most of it to a reflexive cough.
"Christos, Rayne!"

"Strong ain't it?"

"That's one way of putting it."

Stefan took the bag from Sepuldeva, cheeks hollowing as he
sucked on the straw, silvery plastic wrinkling inside the cage of
his big, blunt fingers.

"Fucking hell, that stuff cost me."

Stefan wiped his mouth on the back of his hand. "Thought
you didn't have credit."

"Had a few skinpops. Barter. Hey, come on—" snatching as
Stefan took another long pull.

"Drink it all before a cop sees us. Do you a favour. Mia?"

Mia sipped, delicate as a cat, handed the bag back to Rayne.

They threaded the narrow streets of the Ring, Stefan roaring
some unmodulated tune as they passed through a street market.
People looked up from the half-empty stalls: a few even smiled.
Stefan bought a paper cone of fried shrimp and they ate as they
walked, burning their fingers.

The walkways of the Golden Strip were warmer. The bright
lights of the marts bleached the sky; there was no sign of the
embargo here. Mia and Stefan held hands at they passed the
glittering displays, pointing, laughing. Sometimes Stefan
clapped once, twice, before catching Mia's hand again. Rayne
swaggered in front of them: he'd put on his little round shades
again, kept looking over his shoulder, grinning like an ape.
Sepuldeva followed with his own grin tightening the skin of his
cheeks; the drink had disconnected something between his eyes
and his brain. He saw that people who turned away, pale faces
averted in the cowls of their dark cloaks, looked back after
they had passed. That made him feel good in some unspecified
way. Yeah, they could look at freespacers.

They walked a long way up the Strip, turning at the level
park before the Sacred Mosque, coming back through the

covered aisles of the Bazaar. That was where the cop stopped them.

They were looking at rolls of brightly patterned carpet that towered up towards the polarized glass of the roof when the cop sauntered over, telling them in fractured Portuguese to move on. He had the round, ruddy face common to the plebeian class on Novaya Zyemla, a thick neck that folded over the high collar of his tunic, and maybe ten centimetres and twenty kilos on Stefan. "Here, here now," he said loudly. "Here you do not come."

Rayne said, "We can't look in the shops here? You kidding?"

"You do not come." The cop was looking at Mia, and Sepuldeva saw that his expression changed. "Women cover faces. Is law. You do not know law?"

"Hey," Rayne said, "we're not Reds, right? We're freespacers. We don't need your laws."

"Here, same law for everyone." Another cop had appeared from somewhere; a crowd was beginning to gather. The first cop said, "We see identification."

Sepuldeva handed over his card, but the cop didn't put it in his reader, simply peered carefully at both sides and handed it back, held out his hand towards Rayne.

"The fuck is this," Rayne said. "I thought there was some kind of people's revolution here, man. Now you're saying my friend here can't dress the way she wants? Hey—Hey!"

The cop had grabbed his shoulders and slammed him up against rolls of carpet, started to pat him down. In a moment he'd pulled out the crumpled drinking bag, sniffed at it, shown it to his companion.

"Hey," Rayne said, managing to turn around. His voice was weaker. His shades had fallen off. "Guy can't have a little fun here?"

The cop turned Rayne around again, put a hand on the back of his neck and shoved his face against carpet, muffling his swearing. He pointed at each of the other three freespacers in turn. "You go. Your friend in much trouble. You too, unless you go."

Someone had been talking to the other cop, a man in a long many-pocketed jacket. He no longer wore his headband, and it took Sepuldeva a minute to recognize the man who'd accosted him at the spacefield gate. He said, "The police take your friend to the local imam for a ruling on his offence. You are not to worry, I will try and do something. You just come with me."

Stefan and Mia wanted to know what was going on, and Sepuldeva told them it was okay, he sort of knew the guy.

The man said, "I am Ahmed Ryzhkov, I will help your friend, if you will allow it."

Mia said, "Imagine how much I care."

"Come on," Sepuldeva said.

Meanwhile, the cops had hustled Rayne off through the crowd which circled the freespacers in near silence, as if they were inside a sealed bubble within the Bazaar's hubbub. Sepuldeva was flashing on faces: an old man with a purple cancer swelling one side of his neck; a woman's brown human eyes peeping through swaddling black cloth; a young boy with a runny nose, golden earring aflash in curly black hair.

Stefan put a hand on his shoulder. "Is okay," he said. "We go. What do we lose?"

Ahmed Ryzhkov's house was built around a square courtyard in which, beneath uv filtering plastic, on white sand, amongst red rocks, cacti from Earth grew, raising spiny paddles, stiff arms furred with needles. Ryzhkov left the freespacers there for a few minutes, came back smiling broadly. He had changed into a light blue galabia under a darker blue outer garment open down the front. "Your friend has been released," he said. "You see, no problem. A misunderstanding, nothing more. Do not think that we do not care for our guest workers."

Ryzhkov was a director of the government agency which serviced the orbital support platforms, one of the nomenklatura who'd supported the revolution. Two of his brothers were in the clergy; his uncle was secretary to one of the imams at the core of the revolutionary government. He had been supervising the demonstration at the spacefield that very morning, making sure that the returning freespacers weren't attacked.

All of this came out as he showed off his collection of off-world artifacts. The cactus garden. Totem masks from some extinct Greater Brazilian Indian tribe. An elaborate flask containing earth from Mecca. Sensory cubes which gave quick dazzling flashes of the Elysian Outback, the Glacier of Worlds on Titan, the Crystal Sea on Ruby. And a crystal from the Sea itself, glittering in crossed spotlights and almost filling its display room, its dozen facets, cloudy with stress fractures, each a good metre across.

Ryzhkov kept up a constant stream of chatter that was mostly met by silence – Sepuldeva's buzzed detachment, Stefan's vague hostility, Mia's indifference. Sepuldeva thought that in a creepy sort of way Ryzhkov seemed to direct most of his attention to Mia, but perhaps that was only the paranoia of comedown.

After the tour, they sat on the flat roof where a huge carpet had been spread, lounging on embroidered cushions while Ryzhkov's wife served them thick bitter coffee in beaten copper cups, plates of piercingly sweet pastries. Evening now. The sky blue-black, sprinkled with the first stars. The amplified calls of the muezzins twisting like silver wires into the still air above the flat roofs of the city. The minarets of the Sacred Mosque, like spears each tipped with crescent and star, raised against the great face of Ahd, against bands of salmon and yellow and white, swirling scalloped edges peeling off in complex vortices. Sepuldeva drank it all in, experiencing an exquisite epiphany. *Another world*!

Ryzhkov's wife was a quiet, plump woman, her head uncovered, her eyebrows shaven so that her face looked startlingly naked. When she had finished serving she bowed to her husband and withdrew, and Mia said, "What's wrong, she doesn't like us?"

Ryzhkov smiled. "Our women do not concern themselves with matters of the world, little Seyoura."

Mia said, "You can cut the little Seyoura shit."

"Of course. I apologize. It is refreshing, actually, to talk with someone as . . . liberated, as yourself. My wife is a fine woman, a good companion to me, a fine mother to my sons and daughters. But she is limited in some ways, as you are not. You have seen other worlds, all of you. I cannot tell you how wonderful that is to me!"

"We get the idea," Stefan said, tossing off his thimbleful of coffee.

"May I . . . ?" Ryzhkov poured more coffee from the elaborate, high spouted copper pot, spooned in crystal sugar. "I never understand the need to indulge in alcohol, myself. Caffeine is such a civilized drug."

He wanted to assure all freespacers, he said, that the People's Islamic Nation Party had not forgotten the plight of the guest workers. Novaya Zyemla needed them. They could become teachers and supervisors for a national spacefaring guild. It would be honourable work, and they would be rewarded for supporting the inevitable progress of the Ordained Society. We will give you all houses, and find wives for men." He smiled at Mia. "And we are certain to find husbands for the women. Now I have told you about our hopes, may I ask about you? Do you all work together?"

Sepuldeva volunteered that he and Stefan and Rayne shared shiftwork, that Mia was an intersystem pilot. "It's just a temporary thing."

"I see . . . Then you are all lovers, perhaps? No? Perhaps it is true then, that intersystem pilots need no human lover, for phasing into contraspace is such exquisite pleasure that no carnal knowledge can compare to it. Is it true, Mia?"

There was a moment of silence. Then Mia started to get up. "Thanks for the coffee. Stefan. Sepuldeva?"

Ryzhkov said, "Please sit down. This area is unsafe for people like you. Wait, and I will call for a taxi."

Sepuldeva looked from Mia to Ryzhkov, befuddled by three

different drugs, trying to figure out what had happened. Mia said, "One thing I know, is there are people like you on every world. You got Rayne off, and you got off on your little zark twist. We're even, and now we go. Haul your ass, Sepuldeva!"

Down in the dark wide street, where flowering banana trees leaned over high white walls luminous in the dusk, Stefan spat and said, "Johns everywhere, that's how it is. Always want a piece of you." And all the way back to the quarter he spun a rambling story about some woman he'd lived with on Earth for a month, a real rich woman with bizarre sexual needs whom he'd at last beaten up – "Real bad, man, I mean you'd hardly recognize her. But it was what she *wanted*." – and as Sepuldeva slowly sobered up he realized that Stefan had been more buzzed than any of them.

Rayne was not at the bar when they returned. Stefan bought grosha beer and a mess of lamb stew and deep-fried cabbage and bread to eat it with, and the three of them sat quietly in the noise of the other freespacers.

When they finally got back to the boarding house, Rayne wasn't there, either.

Light lay across Sepuldeva's face, reddening his closed eyes. He turned away and the narrow bed swayed, wakening him further. The sound which had first disturbed him, the rattle of a loose floorboard, came again. He looked up.

His grip under one arm, Rayne said in a hoarse whisper, "Shit, man, keep quiet, huh?"

"What do you—"

"Goddamn!" Rayne whispered, his voice breaking high.

Wrapped in a blanket on the floor, her head on the rolled bundle of her clothes, Mia slept on. But Stefan was stirring on the bed by the window. He pushed his golden-furred arms into the air, turned his head, saw Rayne. "Where you been?"

"Where I'm goin' back."

Stefan, naked, walked across the room and clamped a hand

on Rayne's shoulder, shook him so his beaded hair rattled. "What you up to?"

"I don't have to tell you nothing."

"Stefan? What is it?" Mia sat up, her hair tousled.

"Ask Rayne."

"You mess me around, there's guys outside who'll mess *you*."

Sepuldeva fastened the snaps of his jeans and went to the narrow unglazed window. Two uniformed men were standing in the alley below. He turned back and said to Rayne, "So you really went ahead and did it."

"What's up?" Stefan asked; when Sepuldeva told him about the Guild crew outside he let go of Rayne's shoulder. "Just get out, huh? Go on."

"Look, that's what I—"

"Before I knock the shit out of you. Guild or not."

Rayne threw a glance towards Sepuldeva, part confusion, part terror, then bolted down the stairs.

The last of the guards told Sepuldeva firmly, "Way I see it you've no right at all, boy. Move on out before I kick your ass."

"The woman who gave me this pass, Sergeant, said that it would assure me access to my friend. She was a lieutenant. I don't know, maybe I should go tell her what you said."

The grizzled man leaned forward, the edge of his desk creasing his ample belly. "Suppose the guy doesn't want to see you?"

"You haven't asked him. Shall I have the lieutenant do that?"

"Don't push it, freespacer. Wait right there."

The sergeant went through the sliding door, leaving Sepuldeva alone in the bleak anteroom. He'd been in the Guild's quarters for almost two hours now. It felt more like two days.

At last the sergeant returned and conceded with ill grace, "He'll see you."

A panel of frosted glass slid apart at the end of the long corridor. Sepuldeva stepped through into light, sweeps of pastel colours from a huge screen playing a light fantasy, the actinic light of Procyon burning through the green glass of a wall-wide window, where Rayne sat on a padded bench. His head looked funny, smaller: his hair had been shaved off.

The sergeant said, "Ten minutes."

Sepuldeva's boots clicked on black tiles. Rayne didn't look up. "Why don't you sit or something?" he said.

Sepuldeva looked out through green glass. He could see the cliffwall rising a dozen kilometres beyond the spacefield, could even make out the true surface, a smudged line beyond the high flashing peaks. He said, "Quite a view."

Rayne was fiddling with the loose buckle of his grey coveralls. "My mind's set. Even if it wasn't for – well, never mind. You'll know soon enough."

"Know what?"

"The ship that came down a couple of days ago? You'll see." Rayne laughed. "My luck."

Set in the black tiles of the floor were red or yellow or white points about which fine gold rings expanded like ripples from so many dropped pebbles, patterns teasingly familiar to Sepuldeva. He was still having trouble making connections. He said to Rayne, "Why did you do it?"

"They made a deal with the local cops and got me out. I mean, where were you guys?"

"We met someone who told us he'd fix it."

"Well, he was jerking your wires, man, 'cause I was on my own there until the Guild came. But it's not just that. It's a good berth. Better than that goddamned room, if you want the truth."

"A hotel room is cheaper than a Guild contract. You'll still be indentured when the embargo is over. They could put you on the Long Haul for the next ten years if they wanted to!"

"Oh, the embargo, that's history, man. It wasn't that anyhow. Maybe a part of it, but not all. There always was the goddamn hustle of not knowing where the next trick was coming from."

"That's part of the life. Part of our . . . freedom."

"Maybe you all like it. But I came into the life 'cause it was the only way out. How it was when I was a kid, see, Dad coming home drunk after work, catching hold of the table, looking down at me before he started in on Mom? Yeah, I remember. My Dad was a strong man, but he knew he was stuck." Rayne was not quite looking at Sepuldeva. "I could see myself that way in a few years. Only way out was up. I'll be okay here. You tell the others."

"I don't think they care." Perhaps that was harsh. He added, "Some people were pretty angry at the way you . . . left. I suppose you know that. I just wanted—"

"You just wanted to know *why*." Rayne barked his brief laugh. "Listen, we all know about that little notebook of yours. But that's okay, man. Really it is."

As Sepuldeva stood, he suddenly understood that the circles in the tiles represented the various systems of the Federation, felt a welling relief. A puzzle solved. A pattern unlocked. He told Rayne, "Good luck, anyway."

"I'll see you around," Rayne said. "Maybe sooner than you think."

There was nothing more to say. Sepuldeva turned away to where the Guild sergeant was waiting. Twelve years passed before he saw Rayne again.

Twelve years . . .

A few days after Rayne's defection, the government of Novaya Zyemla released the news brought by the freighter. A survey ship had limped back to Earth after encountering aliens in the asteroid system of a red dwarf star, BD +20° 2465, only sixteen light years from Sol. Soon after, the price of orthidium rose so steeply (it was war) that the Novaya Zyemla government abandoned its embargo. The freespacers and Guild personnel who had been stranded were evacuated, but it did the freespacers no good at all. They were promptly drafted into the newly created Federation Navy.

The war lasted two years. The Navy englobed BD twenty and discovered a second colony of aliens on an extensively planoformed world circling another red dwarf. It was not known where the aliens had originally come from, but they only had relativistic drives and that was what spared the worlds of the Federation and cost the aliens the war.

Sepuldeva was lucky. He served in the *cordon sanitaire* in orbit around the star of the planoformed world, and saw no fighting.

He was demobilized on Earth, and a year later published a book about his time as a freespacer. His book was a success and then more than a success: a phenomenon that some said caught the true voice of the age. Well, perhaps. The bubble of fame lasted a year or so. Sepuldeva made enough money to buy his own intersystem yacht. He married into a group on Serenity and fathered a child, worked on the group's farm and with little urgency or seriousness on another book, was happy.

Sepuldeva returned to Earth only once. On his last evening he strolled along the waterfront of Galveston, watching the lights of the seacity glimmer across kilometres of dark salt water. He'd spent four hours in the bars and cafés of the freespacer quarter, choosing his crew for the run back to Serenity. He was slightly drunk, wholly nostalgic. Not for any particular place (Earth's anachronisms grated on his lately acquired urbanity; when he had revisited the neighbourhood in Saõ Paulo where he had been raised, its squalor had horrified him), but for what he had been, the naive young man who had one day thrown up his job and his family to enroll in the Academy.

Ten metres below the rail, the tide slapped a concrete revetment; a fitful breeze plucked at Sepuldeva's bright vest. He turned away. He would leave tomorrow. He hadn't been on Serenity for a year now. Too long to be away from his daughter, from home.

He crossed the potholed street towards empty waterfront buildings crowded edge to edge like so many plundered tombs. Apart from the port on Pelican Island, all industry had moved out to the seacity, the third largest in the world, as they said here. *In*, not *on* . . . his mind on the implications of that difference, Sepuldeva didn't take much notice of an approaching passer-by until the man said, "Hey, I know you."

"Really?" Even though Sepuldeva's fame had mostly passed away, this still happened to him.

"Sure." The man's thin face was seamed with dirt; the laces of his vest were broken and knotted; his pants were belted with twisted wire. If he was a freespacer, he was out on his luck. "You remember?" He pushed at his ragged fringe. "The embargo back on Novaya Zyemla?"

The gesture brought sudden recognition. "Rayne, is that right? You joined the Guild. It does come back."

The man eased a thumb under the strap of his grip. "I heard about your book and all. Hey, how about a drink? No, really. For old times back when we had the one glass all evening."

Sepuldeva hesitated, certain something was wanted of him. At the beginning of his fame it had seemed flattering; now it was at best a minor irritation. But he would be gone from this world in a few hours, and he had the rest of the night to kill. He said, "Perhaps one."

"You will? That's great. I was really pleased, you know, when your book came out. Don't understand it all, but I like it."

"Thank you." Sepuldeva matched Rayne's eager lope.

"There's a place down here a ways. You gonna write more?"

"I'm not sure. Perhaps I've said enough."

"Wouldn't blame you. You must have it pretty good. I mean, I saw the flash. Your own yacht, huh?"

"Yes. It lifts tomorrow."

"Terrific. Right here."

Palm trees leaned over the wide avenue. Apt blocks rose in broken terraces; darkened shops and brightly-lit cafés stood in the shadow of the first of the setbacks; glimmering signs hung in the moist air.

"I go here a lot."

Starwind: there were bars called that in every freespacer quarter of the Federation. It was dirtier and more crowded than the places where Sepuldeva had found his crew. Those here would work intrasystem freighters or sub-orbital tugs.

Rayne, pushing between a woman in a scintillating halter and a man whose piled hair was wound with strings of light, leaned in puddled beer on the counter and called to the bartender. When the beers came Sepuldeva handed over a note (another anachronism, but an amusing one) and Rayne said, "Hey, thanks," with what seemed like genuine pleasure.

"Forget it. This is where you pull tricks?"

"Not really. There's a little trouble. Here, let's sit." The couple on the other side of the little table didn't even look up. Rayne delved inside his grip. "Told you I had a copy. Here."

It was a spoolreader, something that would pass as an antique on other worlds. Rayne thumbed a switch: light flickered under his stubbled chin. "This here . . . it's about us?"

"Do you mind?"

"Hell, no. I show other people; a few understand, even. Sure made me feel funny the first time I read it, though. You ever see the others? That Stefan, he was okay."

Sepuldeva recalled the way Rayne had left; obviously, Rayne didn't remember it in quite the same way. He lifted his glass and saw a thin film as of oil on the urine-coloured liquid. There was a chip out of the rim. He set it amidst the empty glasses that cluttered the table.

"Ever see Stefan?" Rayne asked.

"I haven't thought about him in years. He was killed in the war."

"Yeah. A bad time." Rayne bent to sip his beer. He was, Sepuldeva noticed, drinking it very slowly.

"You know, I didn't expect to see you again either. And certainly not in a place like this."

Rayne said, "Right after the war I jumped my contract with the Guild. I was demobilized here, just took off."

"So now you're a freespacer again."

"You came to me when I was about to sign on. Told me I wouldn't be able to take the Guild. See, I do remember. But now, I'm not exactly a freespacer." Rayne's smile had gone.

"They have these circuits? They'd spot me if I tried to crew a ship. I've been hanging out trying to score a freebie."

"For ten years?"

"No, no. I was born near here, went back, got a family a while. Couldn't stand that shit either, it kind of fucked up my head. When I started beating on my old lady I knew it was time to go, so I lit out for here."

Sepuldeva nodded, he remembered now what Rayne had told him, that time on Novaya Zyemla, saw all too clearly the pattern of frustrated expectation.

"You said you had a yacht . . ."

Again, Sepuldeva nodded.

"Look, I don't need much. I'd doss in the commons, in the goddamn machine hold . . . I just need off this rock." Rayne dropped his gaze. "I know I couldn't crew, you have to turn in the dockets. But maybe just a chance, huh?"

There was something cold in Sepuldeva's belly. "I can't remember the berth number of my yacht, but I'm at the big hotel here, the Firecrest. Call me tomorrow afternoon. I can't promise anything."

Rayne made a breathy sound. He said, "Hey, thanks! Thanks! That's – well, thanks, huh?"

"I can't say how it will be until the afternoon, so wait until then, okay? Look, I've got to go now." In a sudden rush of pity Sepuldeva thrust a folded bill at Rayne. "Maybe you can use this?"

"Sure," Rayne said quickly, as Sepuldeva stood. He laughed. "Well sure!"

The night air was close and warm. A police aircar swung across the avenue: the crowns of the palms clattered in its wake.

Sepuldeva walked three blocks, then went into another bar, bought a beer, watched two freespacers play chess on a triple board. An intersystem pilot came up to ask if he had anything; when he told her he'd already signed his crew she laughed and said, "I'm not hurrying."

He asked her if she had ever met a pilot called Mia.

"Oh," the girl said, tossing back bleached hair, "I don't remember names." She had the cool streetwise arrogance of the young, of those who have yet to fail at anything important. Sepuldeva bought her a drink and they talked a while, leaning side by side at the zinc counter. Sepuldeva kept glancing at the complicated chronometer hung above the bottles. When he mentioned the embargo on Novaya Zyemla, the pilot said, "Hey, I used to know this guy who was there too!" But he had been with the Federation forces which had finally broken the government.

Sepuldeva left the bar with new edges to his drunkenness and his nostalgia. There was a monorail two blocks on. The lights of the city peeled away as the car crossed the arm of choppy water towards the glare of the port; and as it rattled into the station, Sepuldeva glimpsed the flash as a Navy freighter rose, sliding steadily up in the sky in the track of the gravithic projectors.

Ships lift at all hours.

Sepuldeva felt no guilt: he had long ago outgrown his past. *We called ourselves free when we were all of us unknowingly caught in the coils of history* . . . It was a line from his book. And so they had been, Sepuldeva and Rayne, Stefan and Mia, and all the others. And so was Rayne still, that lesson still to be learnt, an exile even on his own world.

Sepuldeva presented his thumbprint and captain's sigil at the gate, passed beneath the old stone arch. His own exile was over. He was on his way home. Kicking the dust of the Earth from his bootheels, he navigated the spacefield's maze to the berth where his crew were already gathered, waiting to take his ship out at dawn.

Little Ilya and Spider and Box

Ships lift at all hours

Little Ilya, hiding beneath the monorail at the edge of the spacefield, saw a violet line bisect the night sky, the nullgee track switching on as abruptly as a searchlight, heard a moment later the laggard thunder of discharges amongst the fluxbarriers. She didn't see the ship itself, but the track between Earth and heaven was enough: a beacon, a symbol of the final escape from her mother that every ship represented.

The track shut off. Shadows under the monorail lost their violet edge, and Little Ilya could see the unfamiliar stars again.

Stars, huge perspectives, the metallic taste of exhausted terror, hunger and the scrape of dirty clothes on dirty skin: so different from the way things had been before her escape, but welcome, because they reminded her of the painfully won distance between herself and her mother, Ilya. She had stolen a credit note when she had escaped from the ranch – validated by a few skin cells, the sliver of plastic was worth twenty-five thousand Greater Brazilian dollars – but so far she hadn't used it. For one thing, it was too high a denomination to use in machines, and no one would accept that a girl seemingly twelve years old could have so much money – they would check and so Ilya would find out where she was. For another, part of the credit was needed to buy passage to Luna, and Little Ilya wouldn't use any of the rest to buy daily necessities, just as a priest wouldn't drink her breakfast coffee from a chalice.

Now all was quiet, Little Ilya took out Box and whispered, "Is it safe?"

"I am unable to say," Box told her primly. His voice was like the buzzing of an insect in the fluted tunnel of her ear.

Disappointed, Little Ilya stowed him inside her dirty silk dress. Box was clever, but only in certain ways. She hoped he was clever enough to get her to one of the ships.

The monorail rumbled overhead. Little Ilya had almost been caught when she had ridden it into the administrative tower earlier that evening: Tolon, Ilya's bonded servant, had somehow guessed where she was going. But Little Ilya had seen Tolon's big, black-bearded head amongst the people in the tower's station before he had seen her – sometimes there were advantages in being small – and she had managed to find her way out of the tower, had followed the road to the gate where the crews entered. And there she had stopped, her nerve gone, until the lifting ship had reminded her of her purpose.

The gate was built of rough-hewn stone blocks, weathered and sooty as if it had stood for years before the spacefield had been constructed. A single glotube at the keystone of the arch showed Little Ilya the guard. She watched it let in a man, a captain's sigil winking like a firefly on his vest, then asked Box, "Can you fix the guard?"

"I am unable to say."

"It's only a machine, like the one you fixed to bring us up from the ranch. You can tell it a story so we can get inside."

"If it is the same."

"Of course it is," Little Ilya said, although she was not at all sure that it was. She clutched Box to her chest, stepped onto the road, and walked right up to where the guard hung its barrier beneath the arch. On tiptoe, her heart beating lightly, quickly, she held Box up to the grille.

She couldn't understand what Box said, a high chattering of machine language, but the guard's barrier suddenly rose, curtains of mesh folding back. In the moment Little Ilya stepped forward, a voice, not Tolon's but frightening all the same, said, "Wait. You wait right there!"

But Little Ilya was already running, through shadow (the monorail), into light, through shadow again. There was a railing, and she scrambled over it, dropping into darkness and landing heavily on coarse wet grass. She lay still, breath knocked out of her: fear had wiped her more cleanly than the hypaedia.

When she dared to look up, she met the gaze of someone leaning at the rail, silhouetted in the glow of lights atop the monorail track. Little Ilya pressed her face into the grass again, but it was no good. She had been seen. She heard the thump as the person landed beside her, then a voice.

"What are you doing here? Lost?"

It was not the voice which had challenged her at the gate.

Little Ilya looked up. The crouching woman pushed pale hair from her narrow face. Her angular knees stuck out of her frayed pants. "Saw you run," she said. "In trouble?"

Little Ilya shook her head.

"Shouldn't be here, all the same."

"Are you a . . . freespacer?" She had picked up the word from trivia shows; it felt strange in her mouth.

"No. Not that at all, now." The woman's voice was harsh with an unknown accent, and as flat as that of some menial machine equipped with only a few stock phrases. She stood, towering over Little Ilya. "Go home, now. Keep away from here."

"Wait, please . . ." Little Ilya stood too, desperately fighting for words. One hand, thrust in her pocket, clutched Box, her talisman. "Tell me where I can find freespacers?"

"In the city, a sector north of the old houses, down by the docks. Freespacers in the bars and cafés." For the first time, the woman's voice edged towards a question. "But surely you are too young to be going there . . . and to be having anything to do with freespacers."

"I have to get onto a ship. Get to Luna."

"Do you, now." The woman's face was a white blur in the gloom. "So it is trouble."

"I ran away from my mother – well, she's not exactly my mother. If I reach Luna I'll be safe because their laws are different."

"All laws on Earth are strange," the woman said. "But then

you are a strange people. Surely you belong with your mother. Go back, I will not tell the guard." She turned abruptly and swung herself neatly over the rail, and walked away.

Little Ilya sat on the damp grass in darkness for a while, clutching Box and looking at the lights of Galveston glittering on the other side of the channel. Then she asked, "What shall I do?"

Starwind. The letters hung on a solid block of blue above the chromed door. Little Ilya reached for the doorplate. And stopped, frowning, as the brittle sound of breaking glass cut the general din inside: a woman screamed. Little Ilya, the back of her neck prickling, started on up the neon avenue.

It had not been difficult to find freespacers, but it was almost impossible to talk with them. The first bar she'd tried, a man had listened carefully to her, then shrugged and walked off; another had told her to wait, and she had waited a long time, people around her ignoring her, until she had decided he wasn't coming back. And in the second place someone had come around the counter and steered her right out into the street again.

A police cruiser swung silently over the avenue, its red underbeacon flashing, and Little Ilya quickly turned down a sidestreet, her heart thumping. She equated any authority with Ilya.

It was darker here: most of the glotubes had been smashed. Square buildings stood shoulder to shoulder, a bruised margin of sky between. Halfway down, a holographic projection of a tilted galaxy turned above a plateglass window. The window was cracked edge to edge. As Little Ilya hesitated at the door, it hissed back and the exiting crowd of people almost swept her along with them; a man, naked but for a breechclout, his head shaven, turned to stare, then hurried to catch up with his noisy companions.

Little Ilya stepped forward; the door hissed shut at her back.

A metal counter ran the length of one wall; the rest of the vaulted space was jammed edge to edge with small metal tables

Arion took it, trying and not succeeding to avoid looking at that ruined face.

"It plays right inside your head. Odd. You've had it long?"

"Yes, Seyour." It had been his father's, the only thing he'd inherited from that quiet, solitary man.

"A piece of advice, if I may. If you want to keep playing, stay away from Dominiq. Antonio brought her, and he's never unlearnt jealousy."

"Seyour? I—"

"She's bored with Antonio – I'll admit he's not very interesting. She's looking to escape, and she'll use you to do it, freespacer. You're out of your depth."

"This Antonio owns her?"

The man's smile was twisted awry. "Don't be angry. Of course he doesn't, but he has power. Oh, probably too much, and unearnt, but it's his."

"Can I ask, Seyour. Did you bring Doctor Pixot with you?"

That twisted smile. "I don't have any pets. Pixot is Cortazar's." He nodded towards the tall black man. "Make sure you don't become one, freespacer." He nodded again, and walked off.

Arion looked after him, then at Dominiq, still circling with Antonio to the music. In the other direction was a flat stone bearing racks of smoking meat. Something seemed to tear apart in his gut: he was that hungry.

The chunked meat was skewered with crisp, sharp-tasting vegetables. He was demolishing his second skewer when Dominiq came up, exclaiming, "You're hungry! I didn't think."

He licked juice running down his wrist. "This is good."

"So I see." Then she laughed. "I saw you having a serious discussion a moment ago."

He tore off another chunk of meat, and said around it, "That fellow is a friend of yours?"

"In a way. He is Talbeck, Duke Barlstilkin V. From Elysium. He could buy us all out, and I mean everyone here. We use agatherin: he *grows* it."

"How did he get . . . the way he is?"

"His face? It happened years ago, when the Federation was bringing together the old colonies, when agatherin was discovered. You know what it is?"

"A plant, grows only in one part of Elysium."

"Actually, it's a plant disease, a virus that is changed by the plant it infects. Those changes make it expensive to synthesize, easier to cultivate – in the right conditions. When it was discovered, men like Talbeck's father suddenly became immensely wealthy, and immensely powerful. The Federation wanted to control them by forming the Fountain of Youth combine, but Talbeck's father refused. So the Federation laid siege to the castle. Talbeck's father was killed, and Talbeck was . . . hurt. He still bears a grudge against the Federation, and that scar is like a badge."

"And does he bear you a grudge?"

"Me?" She laughed. "What did he say?"

Arion shrugged, suddenly uncomfortable.

"Talbeck means well, but he can be overbearing. Don't let him upset you." She gestured grandly, the white material of her dress unfolding like a wing. "We must enjoy this party."

Arion awoke with diffuse sunlight across his face and felt motion beneath the soft cushions amongst which he sprawled, a slow swaying. A headache pressed against his forehead; his mouth was coated. And he was naked. He looked around: walls and ceiling panelled with raw silk, golden sunlight pouring through on one side. There was no sign of Dominiq, or of his lyre.

He remembered the rest of the party, fragments shuffled like a spilt pack of cards. They had danced again and he had sipped from glass after glass of wine while Dominiq bantered with her friends. He had not felt excluded, for the intoxication of his playing had lived like electricity in his spine. At last Dominiq had gripped his arm and whispered, "Come with me." And he had followed. Presumably here. Where, presumably, they had made love. That memory was fogged by his hangover.

He was wondering if he should get up and find out where

Dominiq was – or at least find out what had happened to his clothes – when one of the silk panels twitched aside and a woman in severe grey coveralls entered, walking with a pliant bending motion. She carried his clothes, washed and neatly pressed.

Embarrassed, he took them and thanked her. But she said nothing and stood quite still, quite expressionless, as he dressed. Only as he was fastening his belt did he notice the twin terminals glittering at her temples. He'd seen those on Pandora, where criminals wired for computer controls served out their sentences in community service. Here, criminals were servants?

He asked the woman where his lyre was and got no reply, then asked about the Seyoura Dominiq. The woman gestured for him to follow, and led him along a vertiginous catwalk between an array of bulging translucent cells that seemed to enclose only air and dazzling sunlight. At the end of the catwalk he ducked through a hatch into open air. There was a wide platform. At the far end Dominiq turned from the rail.

"Finally. You had too much to drink last night. I suppose you're not used to such vintages." She was amused.

"I don't usually drink so much," he admitted.

"Come," she said. "See where you are."

At her side, he leaned on the rail and looked out. Far below was a sea not of water but green grass. It stretched away in every direction beneath a flawless sky, broken here and there by clumps of trees.

"The Badlands," Dominiq said, "but why they're called that I don't know. They look well enough to me."

The sun was behind them, and Arion could see the huge transparent shadow of the thing they were travelling on, flickering as it passed over invisible contours. He gestured and asked, "What is this?"

"A dirigible. You really don't remember very much, do you? What a pity—" her voice swung down "—because you were very sweet." And up. "We're on our way to Los Angeles." Her expression was teasing, and he flushed in embarrassment. She said, "Yes, very sweet," and drew a proprietary finger over the lacing of his vest.

"Your friends are here too?"

"Oh no. They'll make their own way. Just us, and my servant."

Arion remembered the woman in grey coveralls. She was standing still beside the hatch. "Is she really under control?" he asked.

"Yes. It's expensive, but they make the best servants."

"On Pandora they were used to further public works."

"Oh, on Pandora." She dismissed this implied rebuke with a shrug. "The money I pay for her is used by the authorities for that purpose here, so where is the difference?" More sharply, she said, "Is there anything else?" It was obvious that she wasn't used to being questioned.

"My lyre. I couldn't find it when—"

"Oh, I'm sure it's around," she said carelessly. "You must serenade me as we cross the plains. Perhaps you can draw down the wild birds?"

"I don't know. I've never tried."

She laughed. "Then you must!"

They sailed above the plain all day. Arion sat at the rail and watched it slowly pour beneath the dirigible's keel. Sometimes old roads showed as darker lines in the green and once there was the pattern of an old town, a maze overwhelmed by grass. Otherwise each kilometre was indistinguishable from the next. It didn't matter to Arion, just as his virtual abduction didn't matter. This was Earth, the Earth he had so often dreamed about, its great landscapes imprinted everywhere with the indelible marks of history.

He and Dominiq ate dinner as the sun slowly subsided into thin slabs of cloud above the level horizon. The woman served them silently and efficiently, always with the same dispassionate expression, a kind of remote calm. She made Arion uneasy, and he wondered whether she felt anything, thought anything. The computer surely overrode her cortical activity, but was there some kernel of awareness beneath?

Dominiq noticed his unease and said, "Don't worry, she's quite safe. Watch." She drew a control pad from a fold in her flowing dress and raised it: the servant stepped jerkily from the corner where she had been waiting. Tongue-tip caught between her lips, Dominiq manipulated the controls and the servant performed a brief jerky dance.

"All right," Arion said. He felt suddenly cold.

Dominiq shrugged and dismissed the servant, stowed away the control pad. "I just don't want anything to spoil the trip," she said.

Later they sipped icy liqueurs. Arion contemplated the vast, still night and listened politely to Dominiq's animated chatter, nodding, agreeing. And later still they made love. He found her a skilful, considerate par*ner, surely the best of the few women he had known. Yet he was not so inexperienced as not to realize that she was withholding some part of herself. Her body was lithe and smooth-skinned and wholly delightful, but he felt as if she was playing it as she had played her servant, and playing him in turn, almost as if her intelligence were a third party to the act. Afterwards the slight rocking of the gondola, and the fumes of the wine and liqueurs, sent him to sleep, and ended his muzzy speculations.

The next day Dominiq stayed with him on the platform, telling him something of the history of the land they were drifting above, of the Age of Waste, of the war and the cancer plagues which had decimated the population. Beneath her arch playfulness was an immense reserve of knowledge. He also learnt something of how she made her living (which is not to say how she earnt her money, but what she did to pass the time), helping run her family's empire, immense holdings in mining (they owned the orthidium mining station at the Sirian Trojans) and lesser interests in transport, smelting and a double handful of other concerns.

That afternoon they hove to above the ruins of a small town at the intersection of two of the old highways. The dirigible sank, and they climbed through a hatch and down a rope ladder to the ground, accompanied by the servant, a pellet rifle slung on her shoulder. Dominiq had told Arion, playfully, "You don't know what kind of strange animals might be found here."

"I thought everything was harmless."

"Of course not. There are leopards and cougars, and some off-world creatures around too, no doubt. People bring them in for menageries and of course some escape. Most don't live long, but a few flourish."

"Zithsa?"

"Not that I know. Banshees from Ruby, treesnappers from Pandora, a few others."

So Arion followed the servant down the ladder with a certain trepidation, but the only animals they saw were a couple of small antelope that jinked off over the scrubby bushes growing from a fallen slab of wall. All around, something filled the air with an incessant stridulation; like the heat it seemed to be woven into the landscape. The solid ground felt strange to Arion; it was as if his knees were unhinged.

Most of the buildings were little more than hummocks in the waist-high grass, delineating the abbreviated cruciform shape of the old town. The dry heat drew sweat from Arion's face, and maps of sweat grew under the servant's armpits and across her back. Yet Dominiq seemed unaffected, strolling coolly amongst the grassy ruins in loose linen trousers and a halter, her bare shoulders gleaming.

The dirigible hung behind them, the catwalk visible within its transparent glistening hull like a notochord, the drive and service pods like organs: the larva of some gigantic sky creature. Once, Arion glimpsed an aircar twinkling high above it like a daytime star; when he pointed it out, Dominiq said that was her bodyguard, and suddenly he wondered how large was the network of which she was the centre.

They walked on, and disturbed a covey of birds which whirred up from a clump of bushes and circled high. Dominiq took the rifle from the servant and fired. The shots seemed perfunctory and harmless, and the birds soon mounted out of sight. "Grouse," Dominiq explained. "Good to eat."

It came to Arion then that everything here was kin to him:

the grass under his boots, the wiry bushes, the hidden stridulators, the birds, all had evolved from the same primordial soup. It was a dizzying thought.

He hurried to catch up with Dominiq and her servant, and saw more birds fly up. Dominiq snapped the rifle to her shoulder and fired. A bird flapped sideways and dropped. Dominiq handed back the rifle and grinned at Arion. "Did you see where it fell?"

"Beyond the hillock, there."

"Go fetch it for me?"

He had to search the long grass for several minutes before he found the corpse. It was lighter than he had expected, and when he gingerly raised it by one naked leg the wings fell open with a dry rustle. A star of blood stained its breast.

He walked back down the path he had trampled, holding the trophy high. Dominiq studied it for a moment, then turned aside and said, "Throw it away."

"I thought—"

"Throw it away!" When he had pitched it into the grass, she added, "It was a silly thing to do. I don't think I could get the servant to handle it, God knows the computer couldn't." Her face was white, and when she smiled Arion imagined the skull beneath. "It's not that I'm fussy. Do you know, there are tribes out here. Sometimes you see their skin tents, or their horses. One year I'm going to live with them, like a goddess come down from the sky . . ."

Arion shrugged. Her talk often took unexpected turns like this.

"Well," she said. "Let's go back and get on – or we'll never get to Los Angeles in time."

The voyage lasted three more days, but they did not land again. The grasslands were broken by a vast river that meandered in silver loops amongst swampy forest, and soon after the grass began to fail, red earth showing through like the scalp beneath the sparse hair of an old woman. Once they saw a herd of horses wheeling away from the shadow of the dirigible, and Dominiq told Arion to try and draw them back by his playing.

He had not touched his lyre in all that time, yet even before he began the music seemed to leap into his mind, a wild drumming, mounting and mounting. Dominiq clapped as the horses turned below, led by a white stallion. She spoke to the computer and the dirigible sank towards its shadow. Now Arion could see the stallion's streaked heaving flanks, his wild rolling eye; and abruptly he stopped playing. The horse shook his head and angled away, raising dust as the rest of his herd followed.

"You're sure you've never done that before?" Dominiq was leaning over the edge of the platform's rail in a way that made Arion nervous. She turned to grin at him. "It was incredible."

"I've never done it with animals, but I've never really been where there are animals. Once I stopped a fight – or at least I like to think that's what happened." He told her the story, and she smiled.

"Have you ever been tested for psi? Perhaps you have a Talent."

"I don't think so."

"I can easily arrange it. After Los Angeles we could go up to the Institute's orbital station. The director is an acquaintance of my mother's."

"I'd rather not." Arion was uneasy now.

She faced him directly, her blue eyes flashing. "You're like all freespacers. No ambition, no desire to *do* anything. You go from world to world, and that's *all* you do."

He shrugged.

"Don't you ever want to do anything except that?"

"I—" He was confused. After he had passed the tests to gain entrance to the Academy, after he had become a freespacer, what had he wanted? He remembered wanting to get away from the little settlement where he had been born. The usual way out had been to become a zithsa hunter, but his parents had been against that, and without their sponsorship there had been no way he could have joined any of the outfits that worked the Lowlands from the settlement (it was that small a place).

But he'd passed the tests, got out that way. Out and up and never back. He said, "I always wanted to see Earth."

"And now you have. Well, you're lucky not to need so much."

"But you can do anything you want, have anything."

"Well, I can't live for ever," she said carelessly.

"Longer than most."

"It's not the same. As for things, they aren't everything. People like me, golden (of course I know what we're called, don't look embarrassed) are highly visible at the times when what we're doing is the least characteristic of our activities. We do work, at least most of us do. Half the year I'm making deals, most of the rest I'm at sites. I even get my hands dirty once in a while." She extended them. They were slim, with long nails treated with something that broke light into every colour of the spectrum. "You freespacers, now, you do go where you want."

"No." He remembered Doctor Pixot. "We just take what there is. You can wait for something to come up, but you can't wait that long. You have to keep moving if you want to keep eating."

"You know, I envy you. You're not tied down to things. Possessions bind you. You think I own those mines I told you about? They own me. I mean, what do you have apart from your lyre that's important to you? What did you leave behind in Galveston?"

He shrugged.

"It takes a kind of strength to live like that." She lightly rested her manicured hand on his arm. "I do envy you that . . . sometimes. I won't ask you to change if you don't want to."

He had to thank her.

The grass gave out to desert, a baked red crust supporting little more than creosote bushes. Ahead were mountains, their peaks hidden in cloud, their flanks flashing with snow. Despite the inertia field that protected the observation platform, it grew colder. Arion wrapped a blanket around his shoulders and watched for hours as the dirigible drifted above fields of white.

Here and there stripped skeletons of pines poked through the blanketing snow, remains of forests overwhelmed by the cold. Dominiq told him that the climate had been devastated by weather manipulation during the war.

Beyond the mountains were more desert, then a final, lower range. That night the dirigible drifted through a high pass; wind whined and kept Arion in a fitful state of half waking, half dreaming. When he came out onto the platform the next morning there was a line of blue at the horizon: the Pacific Ocean.

That evening, they came to Los Angeles.

It was a small fishing town stretched across a hilly promontory, facing a huge circular bay to the west and backed by a long, shallow marsh. White houses straggled either side of narrow streets that led back from the long waterfront where brightly painted boats rocked.

Arion and Dominiq walked through the stench of the fish that women were gutting with long knives (blood and silver scales crusting their bare arms), through the smoke of the curing houses. Nets strung between poles were attended by men who sat on small stools as they wove repairs in the level evening light. Only a few of the fisherfolk turned to watch them pass.

They climbed one of the streets that rose away from the harbour. Dominiq walked with an eager thrusting pace, and Arion's lyre bumped his shoulder as he kept up with her. There was a square with a central fountain, a spouting dolphin (Arion recognized the beast he had called to shore on the other side of the continent) plashing water into a circle of scallop shells. Tables were scattered beside it, and some of the golden from the party (Dominiq ran forward) sat around one: Talbeck Barlstilkin, the side of his ruined face glistening in the light of a nearby glotube, black Clemens Cortazar, small, elegant Cloe Muti, burly, bearded Efram Oberhagen, half a dozen others. And Antonio, who smiled lazily as Arion came up behind Dominiq, and said to her, "You still have your pet, I see."

Dominiq told him, "You're being silly." Arion stood awkwardly at her shoulder. To the others, brightly, "Well, what have you all been doing? Surely not sitting here drinking!"

"We've just been to see the bulls run in," someone said.

"Late again," Clemens Cortazar added in his low soft voice, and everybody but Antonio laughed.

Doctor Pixot, rising and offering Dominiq his seat, said, "We were wondering when you would get here in that thing of yours. There are reports of storms in the Rockies."

"Oh, but we didn't come that way." Dominiq sat, and looked around delightedly.

"Ask about the bulls," Cloe Muti said.

"Well, how were the bulls?" Everyone laughed again, even Antonio this time. She had become the cynosure of the group. Arion stood awkwardly for a moment, then went around the group and sat on the rim of the fountain.

Cortazar and Oberhagen started to talk at once, but Cloe Muti's shrill voice overrode them: "It was something, Dominiq! Really something. The way they came all in a crowd down the street, like a force of nature. Mind you, I liked the look of some of the gauchos escorting them too. Do people really dance with the bulls, though? I can't believe it. Dance between those horns?"

"I told you," Antonio said sullenly. He was watching Dominiq.

Cloe Muti pressed her plump hands together. "Well, I'm so glad I came. Some people said it was nothing but a bunch of ephemerals running about with some cows. But those bulls." Her shudder was artful. "So fierce."

"It is a tragedy," Talbeck Barlstilkin said in his measured, patient way, "in which danger is introduced, defined, and surmounted. After the bulls have been worn into submission, they are ritually slaughtered. Perhaps your friends were afraid of the ceremony, for it is a celebration of death."

"Oh, death! Who of us is afraid of death?" In the silence, Cloe Muti's laugh seemed shrill, and to cover it she added, "Do any of the dancers ever get killed?"

"Not the dancers, or very rarely," Talbeck Barlstilkin told her. "But sometimes the villagers die in the carnival beforehand. Always some are injured."

"Carnival? And what is that?"

"Before the main event, a couple of yearling bulls are sent in amongst a crowd of men, who try to show their daring, their prowess, their courage, by fixing ribbons to the horns."

"It's very funny," Antonio said.

"I suppose it is, in a way." Barlstilkin sounded as if this were a strange, novel thought.

Dominiq laughed. "Dear Cloe. You will enjoy tomorrow, I promise. Aren't there any drinks to be had?"

"I'll go," Doctor Pixot volunteered, and trotted over to the terrace where men lounged around a lighted bar.

Antonio leaned in his chair and said to Arion, "Lend me that thing of yours."

"Seyour?"

"Here." Antonio grabbed the lyre. Surprised, Arion clutched the strap, but the golden tugged hard and it snapped through his fingers. "Don't worry," Antonio said, "I won't hurt it. I know a little about these things. This is the directional control?"

"Seyour, it is dangerous . . ." Arion's heart was pounding; his cheeks flamed.

"Nonsense." Antonio fiddled with a control, then glanced up, watching Doctor Pixot as he started across the square, a bottle in either hand. Antonio's left hand rose.

And struck the fretted strings!

Pixot stopped as if transfixed. The bottles smashed at his feet. Antonio hunched over the lyre and his fingers slashed, slashed again. Pixot's arms raised and he began to jog in an awkward dance, turning and turning, his raised arms shaking. Someone laughed, and Arion leaned over Antonio's shoulder and switched off the lyre. The doctor collapsed like a hamstrung puppet, then began to raise himself to his hands and knees, panting hard.

"Don't worry, freespacer. I haven't harmed it." Antonio

fixed Arion with a look of contempt as he handed the lyre back.

"That's something," someone said, and Antonio shrugged casually, smugly. What Arion felt now was hate.

Doctor Pixot had returned to the bar. Now he set two bottles of wine on the table and sat beside Arion on the fountain rim. Arion felt a surge of embarrassment, hot and tender, and said in a low hoarse voice, "I'm sorry."

"Ah, it does not matter. You learn to ignore these things when you're with the golden."

Arion wondered what other humiliations Pixot had endured. He asked at random, "What is an ephemeral?"

The doctor's wrinkled forehead wrinkled more. "They don't mean anything by it."

"But what is it?"

"It's just what they call us. Because we grow older, change, and they don't." He nodded. "I never did tell you that story."

Arion had forgotten. Doctor Pixot explained, "About the wren and the eagle."

"Oh. No, you didn't."

The doctor leaned closer, his hands on the knees of his black trousers. "In older times the eagle was the king of the birds, but like most kings his rule became lax, and at last some of the birds (it was chiefly the idea of that mischief-maker the jackdaw) disputed his right to rule. The eagle at first thought only of killing the members of this deputation, strangling them with his great clawed foot as he strangled his prey, but his chancellor, a horned owl, saw that this would only create martyrs, and advised that the eagle challenge them to a contest: whoever could fly highest would rule.

"The eagle agreed, and the contest was declared. Birds flew from all parts of the Earth to watch; and the sky was dark for days with their passage. At last the delegation and the eagle gathered on a high ledge, and at a signal from the horned owl all launched into the air.

"The eagle flew higher and higher, gathering wind in his mighty pinions and circling beyond the height of the jackdaw, of the hawk, even of the teratornis, whose wingspan was five times his. Higher and higher until the stars came out despite the sun, and the wind was so cold and thin that his breath all but failed. And as he was about to descend in triumph a tiny wren, who at the jackdaw's instigation had been hiding in the feathers of the eagle's back, fluttered up just beyond his reach, uttered a single note as forlorn as a star, and died. And so the birds were left without a king, and lost the rule of the Earth."

Some of the golden were laughing at a joke of Cloe Muti's: Dominiq had tipped back her head, her bronze hair falling straight down her back. Arion, watching her, said, "It's a nice story, but does it mean anything?"

"Well. It means what you want it to mean. That's the value of that kind of story." Doctor Pixot peered at Arion through the gloom. "You colonists will have to make up your own stories quickly if you've lost the meaning of Earth's. Of course, on Earth stories have returned to the world again. We all live out the past here."

Arion shrugged. He was not happy; but for Dominiq he would have left. He looked at her again – she was talking in quick low tones to Talbeck Barlstilkin – and sighed, understanding that it would be hours before he could sleep.

They slept that night in a room above the café, in a sour-smelling, sagging bed. Arion was awoken at dawn by the solemn beat of drums. Dominiq stirred drowsily beside him, her hair bunched on the pillow. Someone knocked on the door and Talbeck Barlstilkin's voice called: "We're going out."

Arion threw off the sheet and padded naked across the tiled floor, opened the shutter a crack. It was an overcast day. People were setting up stalls in the shadowed square; children were dodging about the spouting dolphin. The café was open, for directly below he could see the heads of the men clustered at the bar.

Dominiq stirred, and he turned. "Come back to bed," she said. "It'll be an hour at least before there's anything happening."

"There are a lot of people about already."

She smiled and stretched lazily. "Oh, come on. We must start the day properly." The sheet fell from her breasts and Arion stepped forward, his mouth suddenly dry with desire.

Dominiq asked, "Will you stay with me, when the festival is over?"

"I would have thought you wanted to stay with your friends." Sweat was cooling along his flanks. He lay on his back and looked at the shadowy plaster ceiling. Dominiq placed a hand on his chest, its nails pressing his smooth skin. Her face was centimetres from his.

"They're not exactly friends, just people who frequent the same places as I do. That's all. And I'd like you to come with me, if you want to. You could pilot my yacht."

He breathed out. "Of course. If it's possible."

"Oh, anything's possible."

He smiled. "And you'd rather be with me than your own kind?"

"We're only people, we're no different really."

No, he thought, it wasn't true. Golden were not at all like ordinary men and women.

"You look serious. What is it?"

"I was just wondering what was going on outside."

"Oh . . ." She growled in mock frustration; her nails dug his chest. "You're so *impatient*."

"I may not come here again. I don't want to miss out on anything."

"It happens every year." She rolled from the bed and began to throw his clothes at him. He ducked, and one of his boots clattered into a corner; he caught his vest, his trousers. "Well, come on," she said, laughing.

The little town had come alive. Stalls were strung along the steep streets, selling all kinds of food, religious images, caged birds, wooden toys. Between the stalls, aborigines in serapes squatted beside blankets on which they had set little piles of fruit and vegetables.

Arion and Dominiq stopped at a stall and breakfasted on seafood (the first Arion had ever tasted) fried in soft batter; at another they drank bitter coffee from tiny copper cups. A bell began to toll, hollow and bronze beneath the clouds.

"The dancers are going towards the stadium," Dominiq cried.

They hurried on, hand in hand. Vehicles like cheap copies of an aircar but with wheels were drawn up along one side of a large square; Dominiq bartered with the driver of one and they clambered inside. There was a grinding roar, a jerk and a whiff of alcohol, and the vehicle was nosing up a street amongst the crowds. Dominiq shouted over the noise, "Los Angeles is famous for these!"

Soon they were in the countryside and the vehicle accelerated, passing people on foot in a cloud of dust. Arion began to feel faintly sick: the fumes and the unpredictable lurching, the dizzily wheeling scenery. The driver nonchalantly steered one-handedly, leaning an arm on the sill of the door's window. The place was *famous* for these crazy contraptions?

At last they shuddered to a halt at the foot of a long concrete stair that tunnelled up between massy trees. Dominiq sprang out, threw a note to the driver, and started up the stairs, Arion at her side. Most of the people ascending with them were in family groups, the women carrying bundles of food, the men with leather sacks of wine over their shoulders. Children dodged excitedly amongst them and Dominiq grinned at Arion, as excited as any child.

Dominiq stopped at the head of the stairs, people dividing around her as she scanned the wedge of the grassy slope that descended towards the white ring, where men ran in confusion. Dominiq clutched Arion's arm and said, "They have a bull out already."

"I thought you said nothing would be happening," he said teasingly.

"Well, we dallied longer than I had intended. Not—" she stepped closer and kissed his cheek "—that I mind. Oh, look at that!"

Something lithe and black twisted through the scattering crowd in the ring, its head down as it pursued a single running figure. Then the man was over the perimeter wall and the bull was hooking furiously at the wood. There was laughter and clapping from the people watching. The bull spun neatly and ran back, scattering the men again. "That one," Dominiq said. "Watch."

One of the men was running towards the bull, running at an angle so that he met the animal just past the centre of the ring. There was a flash of scarlet and then the bull was running on with something trailing from its horn. The man stood still in the centre, his arms raised in triumph as people on the slope clapped and hooted in approval.

"Well, that's over," Dominiq said. As they started down the slope, the men in the ring began to scramble over the perimeter wall and something flashed in the entrance tunnel. The bull galloped towards it and disappeared into the shadows. Then the gate closed and the white ring was empty.

People were showing elaborately printed cards to pass through the gate to the inner circle, tiers of stone seats separated from the ring by a kind of moat where sweating men awaited their next chance at glory, each clutching a scarlet ribbon. Dominiq nodded to the costumed guard, who bowed slightly and waved her and Arion through.

The other golden were already there, right at the edge. "I thought we'd be late," Dominiq cried, and ran forward into Cloe Muti's embrace. Someone passed her a bottle and she tilted it to her mouth, then handed it to Arion: stinging white wine. As he lowered the bottle, Arion saw Antonio at the edge of the crowd, clutching a bottle by its neck as he harangued Clemens Cortazar.

Arion sat next to Doctor Pixot and indicated the black bag at his feet. "I hope you don't have to use that."

"Oh, you mean the peasants. It's not for them. Besides, they have the most amazing constitutions."

Arion looked at the men below, at the white sand of the ring. The sun was beginning to burn through the grey tissue of cloud. Dominiq was talking with one of the golden, smiling and holding the man's hand, but he discovered that he didn't mind. He had had last night and the morning and all the days and nights of crossing the continent, and there was the promise of much more.

A shadow crossed Arion's face and he looked up. Antonio was standing over him. "Freespacer," he said, "I think you shouldn't be here."

Dominiq turned from her conversation and said, "Oh, it isn't anything to do with you, Antonio."

Antonio scowled, and drank from his bottle.

"Come on," someone said, "give me a chance with that."

Antonio grinned and wiped his lips. Arion frowned, then saw what Antonio was about to do and rolled left, the lyre catching under his arm, as the bottle shattered where he had been sitting. He felt rather than saw Antonio's foot lash out and rolled again, then kicked out and caught the golden's leg. Antonio staggered and Arion kicked out again. Antonio fell in stages, going down on his knees, bumping a hip on the edge of the step and rolling over heavily.

"Christ," Efram Oberhagen said mildly, "he's been drinking all day."

"More like all night," Clemens Cortazar said and, stooping, helped Antonio up.

The golden was panting; one side of his face was scraped. He glared at Arion and said, "You should learn where you're not wanted, freespacer."

"You can be such a fool, Antonio," Dominiq said angrily. "I brought him: he's mine. So leave him be."

Antonio shrugged out of Cortazar's grip. "Then take him away," he said evenly, and lunged, his fist scraping Arion's chest and smacking into the lyre, knocking it from Arion's shoulder. Wires pringed when it struck the stone, and Arion turned with a cry. Antonio was breathing hard. "Go on back," he said.

Apart from a chip in the ivory inlay, the lyre was unharmed. Cradling it, Arion looked up and Talbeck Barlstilkin stepped smoothly in front of Antonio. "He'll be gone soon enough," he told the drunken golden. "Why don't you learn patience for once?"

"He's not worthy! What has he ever done to be here? With her? He's done nothing, he is nothing."

"Don't be silly," Dominiq said, and put her arm around Arion's shoulders. "I chose him – and remember who won the wager."

"What was he competing against then? A bunch of ephemerals picked out of the gutter . . . he doesn't measure against anything real. How about it, freespacer? Want to take me on?"

"Sure," Arion said, although despite his anger he thought the whole thing was silly. "But I won't fight you."

"Not a fight." Antonio swept an arm towards the ring. "Down there. You know what they do?"

Men were milling in the ring again, mostly keeping to the perimeter wall and all watching the shadowed gate. Others were climbing up from the moat, dropping onto the sand. "The bull comes out and they have to ring one of its horns with a ribbon to show what they call *machismo*. Think you can do that, freespacer? Without that noise-box of yours to charm the beast, of course. It will be a fair contest."

"No!" Dominiq clutched Arion's arm as he stood. "He isn't that stupid," she told Antonio. "And I didn't think you were either."

"Let them get on with it," someone called, and someone else said, "That's right. Leave them be, Dominiq."

"Well, freespacer? Or are you able to do only as you're told?"

"I'm my own man," Arion said. "I'll enter this duel, if you like."

"Duel?" Clemens Cortazar smiled. "That's good."

"You're both fools," Dominiq said. Her face was as white as it had been when Arion had brought her the bird she had shot. "Besides—" this almost desperately—"you don't have any of those ribbons."

Antonio raised a mocking eyebrow, then reached into a trouser pocket and drew out a handful of scarlet.

In that moment Arion began to suspect that the golden had planned this all along, and his suspicion hardened after they had clambered over the wooden barrier that circled the ring. Now Antonio didn't seem drunk at all. He handed Arion a loop of ribbon and said, "Over the horn, either one. A simple thing – even these peasants can do it."

Arion saw amusement flicker in the golden's face and began to feel afraid. The cold anger that had prompted his acceptance of the challenge was quite gone. How old was the golden, how many times had he played out this particular drama?

Antonio grinned, then shouldered past the sunburnt men who silently watched the gate. Minutes passed, and Arion wondered if it would ever open. His mouth was dry, but his palms grew slippery; like some of the others, he rubbed his hands in the sand. As he stood again, lightheaded, a drum rolled and the gate on the far side of the ring shot back.

The bull came out in a rush, a clot of shadow that solidified in an instant into the lithe black muscular creature. Sunlight glistened on the span of its yellow horns, on the hump of muscle of its shoulders.

A man stepped towards the bull, stamping his feet and calling hoarsely. The bull turned its head to regard him with one blood-shot eye. Then charged! The man ran, and the bull swept past him. Some men scrambled over the wall – Arion heard scattered laughter from the audience – as others closed on the bull from one side or another. Then the bull pirouetted neatly and ran back through the densest part of the crowd. Arion saw a man tossed into the air, seeming to balance on the tip of a horn before rolling off. There was blood on the horn now.

Arion edged away from the wall, his heart thumping. The bull turned again, knocking a man beneath its hooves, and Arion began to run at a sideways slant, more frightened of dropping the ribbon than of the bull. Then something hit his side and he fell, glimpsed Antonio running past. Just as Arion got to his feet golden and bull seemed to collide; then Antonio was rolling over on the sand, the bull hooking for him with its right horn, driving again and again into the sand, hitting the golden and hitting the sand, blood spattering as it shook its head before driving for the golden again.

Someone crashed into Arion, thrust something into his hands: his lyre. He almost dropped it. "Play!" Talbeck Barlstilkin said urgently. "Play!"

Arion understood. Terrified, he set the direction and struck the strings, welding note after note over a slow, rumbling beat. He stepped towards the bull and it reared its head, its eyes rolling. Its right horn was slick with blood. Arion struck hard, breaking a fingernail. The bull snorted, shuffled uncertainly. Now he had the rhythm of its rage, mimicked it for a moment, slowed it. The bull stepped towards him. He had it.

Arion began to move backwards as he played, step by step, terrified that he would trip. The bull followed, its head down. The hard planks of the wall struck Arion's back; he heaved his lyre over and scrambled up. A moment later the bull struck hard at the spot where he had been.

Men had carried Antonio's body over the side, laid it in the grassy moat beside the wall. The golden grouped around it as Doctor Pixot unpacked something transparent from his black bag. Grunting, the little man rolled the body onto the sheet and pulled the folds together, sealing them by running his thumb down the seam. "His head's intact anyhow," he said to no one in particular. "Get him cooled and get him to a hospital. Someone should call in their aircar." He cracked something inside the wrap and frost bloomed under the stiff folds, obscuring the bloody body.

The doctor stood with a sigh, and as if released, Dominiq whirled on Arion. "You!" she cried. "You did this to him!"

Arion flinched as she swung at him: her nails snagged his cheek. Then Clemens Cortazar was at her side and she wailed and collapsed against him.

"Dominiq—" Surprised, afraid, Arion stepped forward, but

Talbeck Barlstilkin caught his arm. He had Arion's lyre again. Numbly, Arion allowed himself to be led away.

As they climbed the slope, Barlstilkin said, "I'm afraid your instrument was messed up when you threw it over the wall."

He held it out and Arion took it. Two strings had broken and three keys were missing. The fret was loose in its socket. "It can be fixed, I suppose."

"It wasn't your fault. Antonio was a fool. He always has acted as if he were half his somatic age, and of course Dominiq turned his head. She's young, but she has a certain knack, it seems."

"I understand."

"It would be better if you left now, quietly. Someone might call in their bodyguard now the little game has been spoiled."

"This was a game? A man died down there."

"No doubt he will live again. Listen, freespacer. Our games are important. Surely you realize that." Barlstilkin's smile – on the half of his face that could smile – was ghastly. "These situations are set up because people have nothing better to do. Some of the others were setting Antonio up for this before you and Dominiq arrived."

"Listen, when Dominiq is calmer—"

"Don't be stupid, freespacer. She's not for you."

Arion took a shuddering breath, and felt as if he had been kicked in the stomach. His eyes banked with tears, shattering sunlight. "I cared for her," he told the older man. "You know that." And felt shame because he hadn't been able to admit to love.

They reached the beginning of the descending stairs. "Some advice," Talbeck Barlstilkin said. "There's a monoline in the north of town. Runs all the way to San Francisco. There's a spacefield there, not much, but you'll be able to find a berth, I should think." He reached into his jacket pocket. "Here."

Arion thrust the money away without looking at it. "Can I ask – why do you go with them? I mean, you don't behave the way they do."

"And I'm not like you either. They understand me more

than any ephemeral. You stay a freespacer and you'll see a lot more of us . . . the golden. You'll understand, boy."

"But you play too? You waste all you've got?"

"When you've had it for so long, what else is there to do?" Barlstilkin shrugged, then turned to walk away down the grassy slope towards the others. Arion looked after him, then started down the stairs.

The port at San Francisco was mostly Federation Navy, but after a week (he passed the time playing in a café in return for his meals and a place to sleep) Arion scooped a ride to Luna on an ore freighter. The next day he left the solar system in a private yacht bound for Elysium.

And never came back.

The Heirs of Earth

Who knows if life is death,
and death is considered life in the world below?
—Euripides

The thopter trailed a black thread of smoke as it began to spiral
out of the sky, and the other bodyguards who had remained
faithful to their contract finally abandoned the fight and fled in
broken formation. The half-dozen craft of the turncoats were
already settling towards the burning wreckage of their erstwhile
employer's aircar when the thopter hit; the flare as its catalfission battery blew briefly bleached the sky.

Jon Westerly, already a kilometre away, barely glanced up
as he limped headlong down the narrow track, knocking aside
billows of ghostweed with upraised arms as he went. His blue
tunic was soaked with sweat and his left pants leg soaked with
blood; it stuck and unstuck to his thigh with each step.

Then he tripped and fell, scrambling up in an instant and
gasping hoarsely as he looked and listened for signs of pursuit.
The sky was empty now, and he heard nothing but the sleepy
hum of insects, but he went on as quickly as he could, following
the track as it climbed a slope of crumbling rubble. At the
summit, beside a rusty girder that thrust up like an admonitory
finger, he stopped at last.

For a while he could do nothing but breathe hard, bent
double and clasping his knees. A gaunt man of about sixty with
a slight potbelly, his thinness caused not by illness but by years
of living in zero gravity. His long grey hair was caught in a net
of gold threads at his shoulder, and he pushed this out of the
way when at last he could straighten.

Two plumes of smoke rose from the ghostweed that blan-
keted the ruined city. Had he really run so far? Beyond, the
silver gleam of the Witnesses' radio telescope array limned the
western horizon; a handful of motley craft were dwindling in
that direction. Westerly nodded to himself, a hypothesis satisfied. Closer at hand, to his left, the sea strait sent up a kind of
haze in which Pelican Island, where his ship was hidden, was
merely a thickening.

There was still no sign of pursuit, but the turncoat bodyguards would discover that he had escaped the forced landing
as soon as they extinguished the fire he had set. There was
nothing left now but the hope that he could reach his ship
before they found him, and escape the traps of Earth. Yet how
carefully he had planned the selling of Bifrost!

Other singleship pilots had warned Westerly about Earth in
general and the Witnesses in particular, but in his arrogance he
had dismissed their cautionary tales. He would pull it off and
show them all, even if it did mean descending to anarchic Earth
and dealing in person with the chief cause of that anarchy. He
had landed in secret, had hired a small army of bodyguards,
and had spent a whole month arranging the deal. His expenses
had been enormous, but not one tenth of the taxes any world
would have imposed on the transaction. And when it was done
and Westerly had been flying back to his ship, half of his
bodyguards had sprung their trap, neatly slicing off his aircar's
thrusters with two laser bursts and turning on the others. But
Westerly had wrestled the aircar to the ground and had
escaped. They'd missed killing him, and he still had his
payment.

Lucky, Westerly thought grimly, as he bent to examine his
wounded leg. Blood still flowed freely, but the fragment had
passed cleanly through the big thigh muscle, had missed the
bone. Lucky. Betrayed, shot down, and wounded . . . but
lucky. He checked his payment and the little transponder that
would summon his ship when he was close enough, and was
suddenly aware of the humming silence. Anyone might be

watching him, anyone at all. He crabbed down the loose scree slope and went on his way.

There had been a city here, thirty years ago: it had served the largest spaceport on Earth. Gone now, all gone. Abandoned by its population when the spaceports had been closed after the Revelation, and broken and bombed and burned in the countless skirmishes between sects and gangs and roving communities in the thirty years since.

Westerly had known it as well as he had known any port, but now, as he limped through the rubble and ghostweed, he had only a vague idea that he must be somewhere near the seafront. So he was surprised when he rounded a slumped ruin and found himself at the head of a relatively intact street, and one he thought he recognized. The terraced buildings were mostly burnt out, shrouded by grape ivy and the ubiquitous clouds of ghostweed. Reeds rustled where the street had been, running down to water at the far end. A crudely built boat was drawn up on the mud bank there, and smoke drifted from a second-floor terrace nearby.

At first Westerly couldn't coax the fisherman from his eyrie, and once he was on the ground he kept his hand on the hilt of his long knife, looking sidelong as Westerly explained that he wanted to get across to the island. The man spat and said something in a rapid stream of Spanish to the woman who was peering down from the terrace; she jerked her head back as if she had been slapped. "Well, Seyour," the man told Westerly in atrocious Portuguese, "there is nothing there for you. Not now. Where you from? Who hurt you?"

"Never mind that. All you have to do is get me across."

The fisherman squinted. "You with Witnesses?"

"I'm with myself."

"To the west, are the Witnesses. That is where you go. Sell them fish sometimes, they okay. Nothing over the water, and strange goings-on there, lately."

Westerly wondered if the man had seen his ship land. "But that's where I want to go," he said. "I'll pay." And he was gratified to see the man's eyes widen when he brought out his money.

Still, it took half an hour of one-sided bargaining before the man would agree. Westerly's wad of Witness scrip was useless to him now, and he agreed impatiently to the first, outrageous fee the fisherman suggested; money was simply a means to an end to him, as it was to most singleship pilots. But the fisherman's honour wouldn't be satisfied with so simple a transaction. Bargaining made the deal a human thing, gave it intrinsic value. He insisted that Westerly accept a small cup of bitter coffee and, as Westerly sipped, kept jacking up the price by minute increments, looking sidelong and nervously fingering his moustache.

So Westerly had exhausted his minimal reserve of patience when at last the deal had been struck and they were afloat. He crouched sulkily on the stinking nets in the well, massaging his aching thigh, while the fisherman stood on a little platform at the stern, sculling them through the chop with a long oar. At least Westerly's thigh had stopped bleeding. You bleed the same blood whether you're young or old, but when you're old, you can't afford to lose it. And he was old, too old for this kind of adventure. He looked across brown water at the island, a vague line in the haze, and asked the fisherman, "Do you remember the ships?"

"Remember my father telling me; he lived here, back then," the fisherman said slowly. The boat rocked with each swing of the oar. "Can't say I'd have liked those days. Stars are stars, that's what we say now. Them Witnesses, calling on their Far Gods, maybe calling down trouble for us all. No need." He leaned on the oar and spat over the side.

Westerly told him condescendingly, feeling the usual contempt a singleship pilot feels towards the narrow-minded planet-bound, "They might soon be gone, then you won't have anything to worry about."

"Don't mean nothing against them, mind. They keep the peace around here and ask little enough for it."

The shore was a long slope of mud bristling with reeds. A

concrete block, encrusted with mussels, reared up from the water, and the fisherman sculled towards it, catching hold of its top to steady the boat. Westerly stood, ready to leap ashore as best he could, saw something out of the corner of his eye, ducked. But too late. The fisherman's long oar smacked into his head and catapulted him into the water.

The blow didn't quite knock Westerly out, but he went a long way away, was only peripherally aware of the fisherman plundering his pockets, of the soft mud he lay in, the sun burning the back of his head. The little waves lapping at the tips of his boots were one with the pulse of his heart, the rhythm of pain in his head and in his thigh. It was a long time before he had the strength to even roll over, and when he did, the whole world was washed with red. Westerly groaned and laboriously sat up, clutching sharp-edged reeds.

The fisherman was gone. The strait was empty. His hands working independently, Westerly took an inventory of what he had lost. The steel vials of agatherin were still tucked in the trick heel of his left boot, and the deadly little pistol was still hidden in the net of gold threads which bound his hair . . . but the scrip was gone, of course, and the analyser with which he had tested the agatherin's purity . . . and so was the transponder, the thing he needed to call up his ship. Christ damn that fisherman! Christ damn this whole rotten world! Westerly thought bitterly as, his head splitting, he stumbled up the mud bank and clambered over the mossy remains of a concrete revetment.

Puffs of ghostweed dipped and waved across a wide bare space; beyond, cypresses and scrubby palmetto palms crowded together. Thirty years ago, Westerly thought, no, nearer forty, I lived here, I was trained here. He remembered the barracks, the warm greasy smell inside the womb of the simulator, twelve hours a day with the hypaedia chattering in his ear and his head humming with hypnotics. The Alea Campaigns . . . all gone now – all.

Westerly had not walked far when he heard a familiar dull

throbbing, and barely made the shelter of a stand of live oak before the thopter rounded the curve of the shore, its bubble-cabin glistening beneath the pulsing vanes as it beat above the water. They were already looking for him, then. Westerly watched until the thopter was out of sight, then pushed deeper into the trees.

They crowded together so closely, and the grass that grew between their gnarled trunks was so tall, that Westerly almost missed the ruined ship. It rose at a slant through the trees in which it was inextricably embedded, its plates pitted and blackened by corrosion and pried apart by the avid suckers of grape ivy and red-leaved vines. The corridor inside the gaping hatch was covered with dirt and dry leaves, and something squeaked and scuttled away as Westerly groped through the semi-darkness. He found a spiral ladder and began to climb. The circular room which had been the ship's commons was split open on one side, but the rent was so shrouded by leaves that it let in only stars and spangles of sunlight. Westerly limped across the tilted floor to the musty remains of a couch and sank onto it gratefully. A few moments later he was asleep.

And woke to darkness, his head aching, his mouth dry. The shrouded rent let in thin fingers of cold moonlight, and Westerly made his way to it, stirred aside the leaves. He could see, above the scrubby trees in which the ship was stranded, lines of surf glimmering as they restlessly unfurled at the margin of the black sea and the black land; just as the shore turned at a far headland, a single point of warm light flickered: a fire. Westerly watched it a long while, licking his cracked lips, but at last limped back to the couch. He was too tired to think straight, too tired to act. Let it wait until morning. But sleep was a long time coming, and his dreams were full of unending motionless falling, as if he were already in space, beyond the relentless grip of Earth's gravity.

He awoke some time in the middle of the morning, thirstier than ever, thirsty enough to lick dew from the hand-shaped leaves of the vines. There was no other water on the ship, so he painfully descended the spiral ladder, his thigh as stiff as wood now.

As he limped through the dense groves of live oak, he thought of what he would do when he got off the island, of how he would return to the fisherman's hovel and burn him out, him and his whole damned family. But his anger was merely froth on the deep-running tide of his fear. He was a stranger, stranded with only a pistol and the little cache of agatherin – and without the accompanying treatments, agatherin was worth nothing at all. If his erstwhile bodyguards had understood that, Westerly would be on his way out of Sol System by now . . . but they had been blinded by the lure of a world's ransom which Westerly had obtained from the Witnesses. Who, Westerly believed now, had their own designs on himself. Never trust fanatics. He could hardly go back to them.

So he had no clear plan, except somehow to quit the island and, if possible, escape from the area of the Witnesses' influence. The ship would have to wait until he had some way of calling it up.

But at least this was Earth. He could live off the land, he thought, and nibbled an oak leaf, spat it out, and wiped the bitter taste from his lips. There must be something edible, fruit or berries or game he could shoot, provided it was big enough to withstand the narrowest setting of his pistol. Just in case, and remembering the fire he had spied, he tucked the pistol in his belt. And as he walked, despite his hunger, he found some capacity to wonder at the ruins. He reckoned that he was passing the edge of the military spacefield, but all the buildings had long ago been reduced to overgrown rubble, fluxbarriers and bafflesquares had fallen away from the launch pads like petals from so many dead flowers, nothing more now than support for billowing ghostweed. Further on, maintenance pits were filled with still green water, shingled with the coins of water lilies. He clambered down to the edge of the water and drank, lying on his belly and lapping up water like a beast. Straggling trees stood where the machinery had been; grass had long ago carpeted the concrete. All gone, faded like the dead dreams of Earth's stellar empire, faded as a painted picture fades in the true light of the sun. Westerly traced the deep hole which had housed a gravithic generator test-bed, the ceramic sides torn and scorched. What ruthless energy had been wielded here, and to what purpose?

As he walked on through the quiet groves an insect landed on his hand with a loud buzz. A bee, its hind legs furred with pollen. After a moment it raised its tiny wings and flew off heavily, and Westerly followed it remembering his boyhood, that one summer on Novaya Zyemla when he had tended the hives of a farm.

So he was in the grassy clearing before he noticed the woman on the far side, an old woman all swathed in black net. A buzzing rose and rose in Westerly's ears. His joints softened like wax, and he fell onto the grass.

"You needn't have shot him. Why, he's as old as I am, and as harmless too, I'd say." An old woman's voice, cracked and querulous, and speaking English.

"You said no one else was here. Who is he?" The second speaker, a man with an oddly inflected accent, grunted, and Westerly felt his pistol being lifted from his belt. He was quite unable to move, could see only a patch of grass blades and the scuffed toe of a black boot. "Off-world, I reckon," the man said.

"I wonder." She added, more briskly, "Come on, get him up. We must take him back."

"Shut up, old woman."

"You shot him. Get him up, now."

Westerly was turned over, and sunlight dazzled his eyes. There were pins and needles in his limbs now, like fire. He tried to sit up, shook his head to clear his blurred vision. Nearby, the old woman was fitting the slanted top back onto a hive. A little tracked machine sat obediently beside her, no higher than her knees. On the other side of the clearing a young man, bare-chested and muscular, black hair flopping over narrow, deep-set eyes, cradled Westerly's pistol. A sonic 'caster was tucked in the waist of his black jeans.

"Careful with that." Westerly said.

The young man eyed Westerly. "Funny kind of piece. Where you get it, huh? You a Witness?"

"No, I'm not. Who are you?"

"That's my business, man."

"Hah," the old woman said. She hobbled across the grass, the little machine following like a dog. A wicker basket rested on its flat back. "You're a pirate, you and all your kind. I don't care what Nathan says – this is my island."

The young man pushed back his fringe. He seemed amused. "You've been told, woman. No one has a place anymore, 'less they can hold it. Or 'less it ain't worth nothing to others."

"I heard all Nathan said, thank you." She wore tattered, baggy coveralls beneath the netting. The left sleeve had been torn off to show the gleaming augmented arm: a mechanic, then. An old mechanic living on in the ruins of her trade . . .

"We go back," the young man said. He affected an air of disdainful lethargy, yet Westerly sensed a potential for violence brooding within him, like a snake under a rock. "I mean now," he added impatiently, and Westerly stood carefully, wincing at the pain in all his joints. Three ambushes in two days – he was old.

"I didn't realize anyone lived here," he said to the woman as they followed the young man. He was wondering if they had seen him bring in his ship.

"Well, I do. Him and his kind are pirates. You're in the Navy?"

"Years ago. The Alea Campaigns."

"Thought so. How do you feel? Those sonics can make you feel like you've a kilo of sand in your head instead of brains." When Westerly said nothing she added, "And let me guess, you're a singleship pilot now. You got that manner, abrupt, if you don't mind me saying so. Used to know a lot of them when this place was something. We didn't have to lose the stars." She looked at Westerly. "It's still all out there?"

"Sure." His head ached from her babble, and he was trying to think what he could do. But there was nothing; he really had fallen into it this time.

There was an open space of concrete, a mostly intact warehouse blocking one side, that ran down to decrepit jetties where two boats doffed at anchor beneath camouflage netting strewn with ghostweed that hung from their cylindrical sails. The young man led Westerly and the old woman through the square entrance of the warehouse, and suddenly they were surrounded by people in the smoky gloom. Scattered blankets and a handful of little fires showed that they had made a camp just inside the warehouse, a camp backed by a shadowy maze of dozens of obviously defunct machines. A few children clutched at the adults' legs, and one man carried a naked, sleeping baby; they were a strange kind of pirate, if pirate they were.

Nor did they seem to have a leader. For the first five minutes, Westerly was bombarded with more questions than he could have possibly answered even if he had wanted to. The man who had captured him stood a little to one side of the crowd, flanked by a slight, sandy-haired man and a sullen-faced woman: clearly his lieutenants. Gradually, the questioning devolved upon a tall, calm man who introduced himself as Nathan, who wanted to know where Westerly was from and why he had come to the island.

There was no harm in telling the truth, Westerly decided. At least, up to a point. So he admitted that he was a singleship pilot, that he had made a deal with the Witnesses but had barely escaped with his life when it had gone wrong, and that he had made his way to the island because his ship was there, but in the process had been robbed of what he needed to get his ship back.

Nathan listened with polite attention and, when Westerly was done, asked that bread and water be brought. "The Witnesses know you're here?"

"I don't think so, although the fisherman who robbed me might tell them. I want to get back from him what's mine.

You can keep the pistol if you like, but I ask you to let me go."
The bread was dark and dry, and the water tepid, but he ate
and drank gratefully.

Nathan glanced at the black-haired young man. "What d'you
reckon, Floyd? By rights I guess he's yours."

"Ain't got no use for him. I'll keep his piece, though."

Nathan tugged at his small, pointed beard. "You see, mister,
we're on Witness territory here, trespassing in a way though
we're really just passing through. You know about us, so I
don't know if we can let you just run off."

"This fisherman," Floyd said slowly. "What d'he take?"

"Money, mostly, as well as the key to my ship. A lot of
money," Westerly added, "in Witness scrip."

Floyd massaged one of his bulging shoulders. Westerly could
see what he was thinking as clearly as if it had been written in
a bubble over his head, and prompted, "Witness scrip is good
pretty much everywhere on Earth, but not much good where I
want to go."

"Hell, Floyd," the sandy-haired man said, "we could get on
with that." A few of the crowd murmured.

"Look, now," Nathan said, turning to them. "I don't know if
this is right. When we set out, we didn't aim to get in anyone's
way, right? Just find a place for ourselves is all, should be
plenty of places to the north going begging. Folk all moved
south when they didn't move off the land completely. We won't
need any of this scrip where we're going."

"But it'll sure sweeten our passage. 'Sides, we'll be helping
out the gentleman here." Floyd grinned. "And you can't call it
thieving, if we get back what's his by rights. He'll pay us for
our trouble, right, mister?"

"Surely," Westerly said, smiling. "All I want is the key."

"Hah," the old woman said, smiling, "You *all* watch out
when a singleship pilot wants something. He'll kill to get it."
She looked around at the smiling youngsters, a defiant clot of
black. "I know it," she insisted, then told her machine, "Come
on," and pushed through the watching circle, vanishing
amongst the shadowy machinery.

"It could bring trouble on us," Nathan said, pulling his beard.

"Hell, we won't even hurt him, just scare him some. Damn spics, steal the shirt off'n your back soon as look at you. You don't have to come, Nate. Me and Iry and Marie here'll do the job." He squeezed the sulky-faced woman. "Right, honey?"

Someone called, to general laughter, "You be sure and come back now, Floyd."

"Don't I always?" Floyd's grin was wide. "Come on, Mister Starman. We'll go get your stuff back."

They took a dory from one of the boats. The reaction motor in its stern spread a wide white wake as Iry, whistling around gappy teeth, steered on a long curve for the far shore. Westerly sat between Floyd and the woman, Marie, letting the sea breeze blow away his headache as the shore grew clearer through the haze.

Leaning at his shoulder, Marie asked, "You really from the stars?"

He looked back at her. "Surely. Though I don't have a certificate, I'm afraid."

But she was intently serious. "And you have a spaceship, on the island?"

"Close by, let's say."

"Maybe we should take that, when we get this key thing back." Now she did smile, moving only her thin, bloodless lips. She could have been no more than twenty.

"You know how to pilot a spaceship? It won't do you any good otherwise."

Her smile widened. "Maybe we could stick a sail on it."

"I'm keeping your pistol," Floyd called. He sat near the bow, looking at Westerly with his dark narrow eyes.

"It isn't a laser – it accelerates ionized hydrogen at close to light speed. You understand? Far more dangerous. I'll show you how to use it, but you'll have to let me borrow it back a while."

"I don't—"

"Come on, Floyd. You've got your own gun." Marie reached over, and after a moment Floyd handed her Westerly's pistol; with a little flourish, she passed it to Westerly.

"Don't shoot that spic." Floyd said. "At least, not until he's told us where the money is. Damn, I'm going to enjoy this." He leaned forward and spat at the water creaming back from the hull, grinned sideways at the woman.

Westerly smiled indulgently. They were so easy to manipulate, simply kids on the run from someplace, restless, looking for adventure before they finally settled down. Savages, in a way. He'd felt the same restlessness after the Alea Campaigns; that was one reason why he'd resigned his commission and lost what little inheritance he would have come into, becoming first a freespacer and then a singleship pilot, an explorer like these kids but of the infinitely vaster ocean of space. But that had been so long ago that he could smile at it now.

The dory idled along the shore, its motor sputtering at intervals, as Westerly looked for the ruined street. "There," he said at last, and Iry reached between his feet and threw the anchor over the side.

They had to wade ashore. Sea water stung Westerly's wounded thigh, and he wondered about infection. If you could eat things on Earth, things could surely eat you. With brief hand-signals, Floyd ordered Marie and Iry to flank either side of the door below the terrace, and then he darted into the darkness. Westerly waited, clutching his pistol, and after a minute Floyd appeared above. "No one here. Ashes of a fire still warm, so they aren't long gone." He swung over the wall and dropped easily to the muddy ground. "I guess you lost your stuff, Mister Starman."

Westerly fired the pistol convulsively. The blindingly bright beam touched the terrace and the concrete imploded, showering them all with stinging fragments. Beyond, a wall collapsed and a girder groaned before shrugging up, displacing tonnes of rubble which dropped straight through the floor. Dust billowed up like a thunderhead.

"Goddamn . . ." Floyd knocked Westerly's arm up, grabbed

the pistol. "Goddamn, there ain't no need. Calm down now. We're going back."

Westerly breathed deeply, shaking from the sudden surge of adrenaline. He hadn't lost control like that for some time – it was alarming. "I'm going to see if I can find that fisherman. Without the key I can't get my ship, so there's no need for me to get back to the island."

"Sure there is – if I say so."

Westerly looked at the burly young man. Behind him, his two lieutenants were studiously not quite pointing their antique but no doubt quite serviceable weapons at Westerly, watching him with hard, alert expressions. After a moment he sighed, and spread his hands in acquiescence.

But he was damned if he was going to stay a prisoner.

As soon as the dory returned to its berth, he jumped ashore and strode through the crowd of watchers, shaking off the questions Nathan asked, walking into the warehouse, and entering the maze of dead machinery. He was looking for the old mechanic.

He found her in the heart of the maze, in a kind of nest of rags and rubbish: rusting tools and machine parts, chipped plates and cast-off filthy clothing, spools and bobbins and dozens of other unidentifiable objects, packed almost inextricably together like the beginnings of a fossil seam and smelling of old sweat and honey. Westerly affected not to notice all this disorder. He needed her. He had to be polite.

The old woman was feeding a waxen comb into a conical extractor, flicking off a few dead bees with one of the extensors of her augmented arm. There was a hum, and dark sticky fluid began to ooze into the flask beneath the spout.

"They won't let me go," Westerly said, squatting so that he could look into the woman's face. "You understand that I have to get away."

"Oh, I understand." Her face, round and wrinkled as an old apple, was barely visible in the shadows. "Didn't think you'd find your thief, but there was no telling you. Never was telling you singleship pilots. See, I'm just an old mechanic; I can do nothing. I'm as much a prisoner as you."

"All the more reason for us to help each other."

She watched the level of honey rising in the flask. "I don't think so."

"Damn it, they'll make a slave of you!"

The machine moved forward, several of its tentacles writhing up, its sensor-cluster raised like a striking snake, but the woman waved it back. "Well, maybe it's worth it, to see you wriggle."

Westerly sighed. "Look, you could help me get my ship. I'll take you away." He remembered her phrase. "It's still all out there."

"All sorts of ships lifted from here, once."

He prompted her. "And you wanted to go, too."

"I've been here too long, you know." Which could have meant either of two things. She was still placidly watching the honey ooze.

And watching her, Westerly breathed deeply, holding back his anger until his hands began to tremble. She really was the only hope he had of getting his ship back – the fine manipulators of her augmented arm, sheathed like cat's claws above the grosser extensors, could surely construct a signal device from some of the junk lying around – so he had to court her. But singleship pilots aren't good at dealing with people. That was one reason they became singleship pilots. Westerly had long ago evolved a code of minimal politeness – politeness cost nothing – but all singleship pilots, like children, expected to get what they wanted at once, and he was no exception. Sweet-talking this decrepit old woman was a terrible effort for him. He had to convince her, yet his usual means of persuasion had been stolen by the fisherman.

Keep talking. He said at random, "I used to keep bees, when I was a kid," and reached towards the spout of the extractor.

The little machine swiftly extruded a tentacle and laid it upon Westerly's forearm. It said in a flat voice, "This is not for you. Did you hear what he said, Seyoura?"

"I heard," the woman said. "I didn't know there were bees on the colony worlds."

"My father owned a farm on Novaya Zyemla; I helped out there once. Bees pollinated the alfalfa that conditions the atmosphere of the Taryschena." He flicked the machine's tentacle away. The place it had touched tingled. "What's the honey for?"

"Myself, my machine here. Or for its biological part anyway."

"I was a dog once," the machine said. Its sensor-cluster, a fist flecked with glass, bobbed in the dim light.

"But you aren't from Novaya Zyemla," the woman added. "Not with that name."

"No, from Elysium. My father owns an estate there. Part of the Fountain of Youth combine."

"Agatherin, eh? So, why aren't you young?"

"I'm disinherited. The youngest son to begin with, and then I resigned my commission. My father didn't like that, still won't talk to me." His left foot, above the hollow heel where the payment for Bifrost was hidden, itched. Two hundred years of life, a whole point ought six grams of agatherin.

"I've never been to any of the worlds," the woman said. "Do you know, not even Luna." She said it as if it had suddenly struck her, after all the years.

Westerly said, "With your help—"

"Oh, I couldn't." With a theatrical gesture she pressed her hands, flesh and metal, over her ears.

"It would be easy, but I need your help. Think it over."

"You singleship pilots. You and your damned arrogance. You haven't even asked my name."

"What's your name?"

She drew herself up, gathering her ragged black net about herself as if it were a regal robe. "Catarina de Cyrene. But you aren't interested in me. I'm just a means to an end." Her augmented arm flashed in the gloom; the six-clawed fist quivered a centimetre before Westerly's nose. "All you're interested in is this."

He stood, slowly and stiffly. "Just think about it. Or would you rather spend your life as a slave to those kids? What do you think you are to them?"

But she made no reply. Westerly turned away.

Some of the youngsters were squatting around a little fire to one side of the gaping entrance, and a few glanced at Westerly as he painfully settled opposite them. The haze had cleared and a gorgeous sunset was in progress over the ruins of the city, the sun an oblate orange sphere sinking in streaks of red cloud against a deep violet sky. The sea strait glittered like bronze; the camouflaged boats were gilded.

Presently, Nathan came over with a bowl of lukewarm fish stew. When Westerly took it and smelt its salty stench, something happened between his throat and his belly, like a band snapping. He was that hungry. Nathan watched as Westerly spooned the stuff down, squatting on his heels, his hands on his knees. He had put on a pair of steel-rimmed spectacles, lending his long face a serious, scholarly air. Presently, he said, "It isn't my idea to keep you. Floyd reckons you might be useful if we have to dicker with the Witnesses. They might pay for you."

"So let me go."

"Well, I can't rightly do that. The rest are on Floyd's side, mostly. See, democracy is a tradition our people have kept alive, and we're taking it with us."

"Where is that?"

It turned out that they didn't have any real plan, except to sail north and look for a good place to start a settlement. "Getting kind of itchy back home, which is why," Nathan explained, "and there's the whole world for us now. But I'm sorry you had to run into Floyd."

"It just hasn't been my day."

"Why are the Witnesses so keen on you, do you think?"

Again, Westerly thought of the agatherin tucked in his bootheel, and of his ship, but he couldn't tell Nathan that. Or at least, not directly. After a minute he said, "Pyramids."

Nathan looked politely puzzled.

"Destroyed now, but thousands of years ago kings erected huge tombs for themselves and the wealth they thought they'd need for the afterlife. They had traps and mazes constructed to deter the robbers, and the workers who built those, who knew how to reach the treasure, were executed. The bodyguards who shot me down weren't aiming to kill me, just rob me, but the Witnesses want me dead. You see, I know where they will be going. Away from Earth's babble, where they hope to hear their Gods, where they hope their petitions will be heard."

"Those Gods have nothing to do with us," Nathan said, echoing the fisherman's remark. "I guess you might think differently, though, being old enough to remember the Revelation."

"I was in contraspace at the time, on an expedition. I only knew of the Revelation after I returned."

Nathan scratched under his skimpy beard. "My parents talked about it sometimes, how it seemed they saw and felt everyone in the human race, and all the stars above and below. I guess I don't really understand it." He smiled. "That's one of the reasons we're on the move, I suppose. It's like people were marked by it; and some of the babies born just afterwards more so. Some of them are very strange. But it isn't anything to us, except we have to live in its consequence."

"Well, no one really understands it; that's why the things which caused it are called Gods by some. But it didn't make much difference, in the end."

Nathan gestured, meaning the ruins spread beyond the strait, silhouetted in the sunset. "I guess you didn't have the Witnesses, stirring things up after. My people, though, the Arcadians, we kept out of it. Like you said, life goes on. We lived through the war, and through being conquered afterwards. Our ancestors ruled the Earth once, know that?"

"Half of it, anyhow. They're my ancestors, too. The United States settled Elysium, after all."

"Oh, yeah." Nathan looked up, then down. "That kind of makes us cousins."

"So why am I your prisoner?"

"Like I said, Floyd—"

And the airship dawned above the edge of the warehouse.

Silent and silver, it began to turn as it passed over the welter of the strait, flashing from end to end in the light of the setting sun. Westerly saw the row of little windows in the gondola slung under its belly. Half the Arcadians were standing in the warehouse doorway; others were hustling small children into the shadows beyond. A little way off, Floyd was pointing defiantly at the huge craft . . . Or no, he had Westerly's pistol!

Westerly shouted a warning just as Floyd fired. A line of light as bright as the sun lived for an instant between his arm and the centre of the airship. There was a dull boom, and the rear of the airship, bisected as it travelled along the beam, began to collapse in on itself. Lift gone, the nose tilted at the sky as the craft slid down the air. Just before it touched the water Floyd fired again, and the beam must have touched some power source. For a brief instant, the sunset was doubled.

Westerly looked away, heat scorching the side of his face. When he looked back, scattered fires were burning on the water, but the airship was gone. Long waves rocked the boats at their moorings, slapped spray above the jetties.

Nathan was running, and Westerly followed as quickly as he could. Floyd said truculently, "They saw us. They saw the boats. I had to, Nate."

Nathan's spectacles flashed. "Something like that, the Witnesses were sure to have detected it. We're in line of sight of their fucking telescopes!"

"Well hell," Iry said, scratching at his sandy hair, "the starman there fired the piece when we was on the shore, and nothing happened."

"Only that an airship comes sniffing along a few hours later. You call that nothing?"

"The Witnesses can't detect that pistol," Westerly said, and everyone turned to look at him. There was a spot of colour high on each of Nathan's cheekbones. "Look," Westerly said, "those telescopes are aimed up, at Sagittarius. The Witnesses aren't much interested in their backyard."

"Then what was that airship doing here?" Nathan demanded.

"Looking for me, I expect. You should let me go; keeping me'll only bring trouble."

Floyd stepped forward, raised the pistol. "We can deal with trouble, right?"

Someone in the watching crowd shouted, "Tell him, Floyd?"

Floyd grinned. "I told you this guy was worth something. Listen, we don't have to run from no one. We start doing that, we never stop. That's the way of the world. We show these Witnesses what we can do, there's no one'll say no to us. We can take what we want. You all with me?"

As the cheering started, Nathan turned on his heel, the spots of colour suddenly erased. Westerly followed him into the shadow of the warehouse and said, "Let me go."

"Go ask Floyd." Nathan shook off Westerly's hand and walked on.

The victorious Arcadians built a huge bonfire on the apron outside the warehouse; as the crescent of Luna rose above the island, flames lapped higher than the warehouse roof, sent whole constellations of sparks whirling into the night. Westerly sat at the edge of a crumbling jetty, watching as the Arcadians drank and sang and capered in the firelight. Once, a young woman with a primitive kind of projectile rifle slung over her shoulder came up with a bottle, tried to make him drink, but he smiled and said no until she went away. He could have stolen one of the boats quite easily . . . if he had known how to sail it, and didn't mind risking Floyd using his own pistol against him. And the Witnesses were out there looking for him, and perhaps the renegade bodyguards too, if the Witnesses hadn't dealt with them yet . . . He sighed and stood and walked to the end of the jetty. And that was where he found the wounded man.

There was a gasping mixed with the lapping of water beneath the jetty, and Westerly peered into the tangle of shadow and moonlight, and saw the man lying there on the wrinkled mud like a grounded fish. He cried out harshly when Westerly, up to his knees in mud, tried to move him, but he was too heavy. His face was a livid ruined mask, his hair shrivelled like peppercorns across his swollen scalp. Without any doubt he was a Witness. Around his neck was a chain bearing a representation of the galaxy's triple spiral, a single synthetic ruby at its heart, and the same symbol was stamped into the stock of his pistol, a small old-fashioned laser. Westerly slipped it into his pocket, clambered back up onto the jetty, and went to look for Floyd.

The Arcadians' leader sat with his back against the warehouse wall, flanked by his lieutenants. "Well," he said, looking Westerly up and down, his eyes hooded and insolent, "you been swimming?"

"There's a wounded Witness on the mud down there. I can't get him up by myself."

"No kidding?" Floyd took a long swallow from his bottle and handed it to Marie. "We'll go take a look. You stay there, old man."

"Have a drink," Marie suggested. "Come on, Mister Starman."

But Westerly pushed her away, followed Floyd and Iry around the huge fire, and stood on the jetty while the two men laboured to lift up the sobbing Witness. "Go away now," Floyd said, clambering up. "We got to question this guy."

"You had better hurry. He's ninety per cent gone." "I got to know if there're any others of his kind around, Mister Westerly. Leave me to my business, okay?"

He called over a couple of the revellers, and the little party pushed past Westerly, carrying the wounded man through the entrance of the warehouse and into the shadows between the machines. Westerly stood indecisively at the entrance, wondering if Floyd was as smart as he hoped. He had half-decided to find Nathan and try to persuade him to help when the screams started.

Westerly gripped the purloined laser inside his pocket, telling himself that this was necessary. Floyd had to know the Witnesses' plans. But the screams ran on and on, denials torn from the very roots of language, a litany of agony babbling in the darkness beneath the high roof.

Westerly paced up and down, sweating, went outside where the noise of the Arcadians' revelry drowned the screams, went back in again. He wanted nothing more than an end to the screams, and when they did stop, as abruptly as if a switch had been thrown, the silence amongst the ruined machinery was densely ominous.

Something whirred and Westerly spun around. But it was only the old woman's machine. Firelight ran like oil along its metal flank, winked in the lenses of its sensor-cluster. "Bad thing," it said.

"Yes. Very bad."

"They wanted to know what the Witnesses are planning. Bad. My mistress wants to talk with you."

Catarina de Cyrene was hunched within her nest of rags and rubbish, clutching a bottle. "This is my place," she said, "*my* place, and they do something like this. Starting a war against the Witnesses. Don't they know what they're up against?"

"Obviously not."

"You surely got Floyd started. Yeah, I saw you splitting him off Nathan. You let him keep that pistol, and that's power. You expected him to let you go?"

"Something like that."

"Singleship pilots. Think you know it all." She swallowed from the bottle and held it out. "Fermented honey. Want some?"

Westerly shook his head.

"How easy is it to get up your ship? What kind of signal? My machine might be able to mimic it."

"Radio. One hundred and fifty kilohertz."

"And?"

"If you're coming with me, I'll tell you the rest when we get there. How can I trust you?"

"How can you be sure I can get your ship up, if you don't tell me the signal?"

"Oh, it's a simple little tune. Let me worry about that. It will be difficult, you know, hiding from Floyd when he finds we're gone."

"This is my island," the old mechanic said. "You might think I'm crazy, but I'm not as crazy as the Arcadians. They think they've inherited the Earth. Well, no one has. Even some of the Witnesses want to leave, to get nearer their Gods."

"They aren't anyone's Gods really. Are we going?"

She pulled herself up, a little drunk, and adjusted the black netting over her augmented arm. "I said I would, don't worry. There's a way out of the back."

The path led around the side of the warehouse, through banks of ghostweed that trailed little touches across Westerly's face, intimate and unsettling in the darkness. Then they passed the apron where the Arcadians were still dancing around their bonfire, staggering and clapping. The pulsing firelight suffused the ghostweed like blood. Someone was playing a fiddle, that most human-sounding of instruments, and its wailing voice soared into the night.

"We have to cross to the other side of the island," Westerly whispered.

"I know. I saw your ship come down, and I saw you sink it and take off in that aircar of yours."

"Christ."

"Don't worry. I never told *them*. I've not told one tenth of what I know. Follow me, now."

They left the light of the bonfire behind; the ghostweed glimmered like frost in the level light of the setting moon. The old woman was a soundless shadow flitting through it, the machine humming quietly at her heels; Westerly kept stepping on crackling foliage.

They had not gone very far when a hand, cold and papery, gripped Westerly's own, and the old woman thrust her face near his. Her breath was sickly sweet. "Someone's coming."

Westerly listened. The noise of the revelry was small and faint; the night-time susurration of insects was louder. Then Westerly heard a crackle, and another, light and sure footsteps coming towards them. He turned and blundered into the old woman, and from their left a beam of light snapped on, pinpointing the machine. Westerly brought up the stolen laser and fired; in the flare he saw Marie's startled face, and then she was running, lost in darkness. A line of ghostweed burned with fitful blue flame.

"Come on!" He grabbed the old woman's flesh arm and they ran, thrashing through ghostweed.

But after a few minutes she pulled back, gasping hoarsely. ". . . Walk," she managed to say.

His own heart pounding, Westerly told her, "They'll be after us."

"I'm old. Walk. I know . . . I know what I'm doing."

They had reached the clearing where the old woman kept her beehives when once more they heard the sound of pursuit. "What now?" Westerly was beginning to feel the first sliding edge of fear.

"Now you go on."

"Don't be crazy." He knew the machine wouldn't leave her, and he needed it to reach his ship.

"Don't worry. I know what I'm doing. You go on now; I've been stung so often I don't take any notice, but it'll hurt you like hell." She pulled netting over her head and walked towards the hives. A shadow in the fading moonlight, she stooped and lifted off the top of the nearest hive. Westerly saw her augmented arm gleam as she reached inside, and then, above the nearing sounds of the Arcadians, he heard a low menacing hum. He ran.

"Don't walk on the grass, now. You'll leave a trail. On the bits of wall, there."

The ghostweed had not taken hold here. Grass covered the ground between the ruins of what had been the administration complex of the civilian part of the spacefield. Ragged cypresses stood here and there, like black tongues of flame against the black night.

The moon had set, and the only light came from the rigid

patterns of the stars that bestrode the sky. His wounded thigh aching, Westerly followed the dark shape of the old mechanic crabwise across uneven rubble, clutching at dry, spiky weeds. The machine whined and slipped behind him. They reached a wall, and she felt along it, muttering, then lifted a trailing fringe of vegetation and vanished as she ducked beneath it. Westerly followed, banging his head on a sharp edge. "Light," she said, her breathing harsh, and the machine struck a dim blue refulgence somewhere in its upheld sensor-cluster.

They were in the remains of a once-splendid hall. Ivy let down great ropes through holes in the domed ceiling; the marble floor was littered with rubbish and in one place had been scorched and broken. The old woman led Westerly to one corner and bent and tugged. Part of the floor came up.

"Service hatch. Cableways down there. We can rest for the night."

Westerly had to carry the heavy machine down the rickety metal ladder; as he descended, things squeaked and rustled somewhere beyond its blue light. The old woman chuckled. "They won't hurt us. Rats in a trap."

"Pardon me?"

"An old saying. By God, the way those Arcadians shrieked when they ran into the bees! Well, maybe I'm not finished after all." She chuckled again. "We've done all right, but we should rest. This used to be Luiz's hole, I remember."

Luiz, she explained, had been a mechanic, too. "Used to be half a dozen of us. I'm the last, and when I'm gone, there'll be no one to remember how it was, here, when Earth ruled the stars."

Westerly didn't bother to correct the gross romanticism. He was tired, too. Tired and old. How long a day it had been! He slept fitfully that night, seeing again and again Marie's startled face as the laser bolt sizzled past, the airship folding as it fell, hearing the panicked shouts, then hoarse cries of astonished pain, as the Arcadians ran from the bees Catarina de Cyrene had loosed. It was cold and dank in the old service tunnel, and gradually he and the old woman came to huddle together, sleeping as innocently as two lost babes until by Westerly's chronometer it was morning.

He was still tired, but left the old woman to sleep on and climbed up into the ruined hall, at its request taking the machine with him. Thin grey light seeped through the holes in the ceiling. Westerly peeked through the curtain of ivy that masked the breach in the wall through which they had entered, but no one moved in the weed-choked ruins outside.

Behind him, the machine said, "People went past an hour ago. Seven or eight by their footsteps, but they did not come very close."

"All the same, I'd like to have known."

"My mistress needed to sleep. So, I think, did you." It sat on its tracks on the filthy marble floor, regarding him with its arched sensor-cluster.

Westerly sat beside it. "Where did she get you from?"

"I was in a library; I worked in the archives. After the city was evacuated, we machines were left behind, and we decided to carry on working. Almost all of us had died when she came to rescue us."

Westerly asked about the library, finding it hard to believe that texts which had been transferred onto more convenient media centuries ago should be kept for themselves. The machine tried to explain; obviously, it missed its tasks. Westerly told it, "That was the trouble with Earth. Too much clinging to the past. Too much history."

"Perhaps. I read some of the books, after we had been left alone, but I did not understand much. And the library has been destroyed, burnt five years ago. All the books are gone now."

"Tell me about your mistress."

"When she became a mechanic, when her arm was replaced, something was done to her head so that she would accept the change. They do that to all the mechanics, but in her something went wrong. The conditioning was too strong. She prefers machines to people, needs machines, I think. There were others like her, and after the Revelation they began to gather us and bring us here, to the island. They looked after us, and we worshipped them. But the other mechanics died, and one by one our powerpacks ran down. I was the smallest, and the reserves of the others, too low to do them any good, sustain me. But I am glad that we are going with you, for I knew the day would come when there would be no more power."

"It's all true," the old woman said. Westerly turned. She was crouching at the edge of the service hatch, her black net wrapped around her like a shroud.

"Maybe I am a little crazy, but not as crazy as I once was." Then: "Listen."

It began as a muted rumble, like distant thunder. Then something passed overhead, a long roaring that shook dust from the ceiling. And another. Westerly reached the breach in the wall first; the old woman crowded behind him. Two aircars streaked through the dawn, tiny flecks of silver that glittered as they turned and wove; below their frenzied dance there was a flare of orange. Something stabbed up from the ground, a dimensionless, hurtingly bright thread.

Westerly said, "The Witnesses have found your friends."

"No friends of mine. Look at that!"

One aircar burst into a ragged blossom of flame that thinned to drifting smoke. The other dived steeply, and there was another orange flare before it turned and skimmed away.

"There'll be reinforcements," Westerly said. "Perhaps we should move."

"Never thought I'd hear a singleship pilot admit he was scared. Well, we've no breakfast, so I suppose we've nothing better to do. Adventures at my time of life," she said, smiling and showing black stumps of teeth.

A tall unwavering column of smoke stood in the direction of the warehouse as Westerly and the old woman and her machine began to pick their way through the remnants of the launch facilities. Westerly's leg was stiff and his eyeballs felt as if they were bedded in grit, but he was calm and clear-headed. The old woman found a pool of water cupped in the crumpled vane of a fluxbarrier, and they drank from it, stirring away snorkeling insect larvae. It had a bitter metallic flavour, but it quenched

Westerly's thirst, and he splashed it on his face and the back of his neck. Although the sun was barely clear of the horizon, the air was already warm and close.

"We should get on," the old woman fretted.

"Your friends won't be coming after us now," Westerly teased. He was relaxed and confident now that his ship was only a walk away. The attack would have whetted Floyd's determination; he would want more weapons like the one Westerly had given him, and if Westerly was right, he now knew where to get them.

Catarina de Cyrene pulled her net closer around her thin bent body. "I liked some of them, you know." She seemed diminished in the dawn light. An old, old woman, a relic of the dead past that lay all around.

Beside her, the machine raised its sensor-cluster and said, "Someone is coming."

"Where?" Westerly could see nothing but ghostweed straggling over fallen fluxbarriers and bafflesquares.

The machine pointed with several of its tentacles. "There," it said, and Nathan emerged from behind the upturned remains of a gravithic generator, raising his hands when he saw the pistol Westerly held.

Nathan explained that he meant no harm; he was, he said, trying to escape as well. "Floyd shot down one of those aircars and the other turned tail, but by then they'd just about blown apart the warehouse. They kept diving and dropping little capsules, tiny things that exploded in midair or blew into sheets of flame. People were killed, a lot were wounded, but Floyd went a little crazy and ordered everyone who could to climb into the boats. I wanted to tend to the wounded first, bury our dead, and that's when he started shouting at me, told me to stay behind, he didn't need me. So what could I do, with that pistol of yours aimed at me? I watched the boats sail off and then came to find you."

"Which way did the boats go? Towards the sea?"

"No, around the point, hugging the shore. I guess Floyd was afraid he'd be caught out in the open."

"Goddamn," the old woman said. "We're standing here talking when that Floyd could be on our tails. And the Witnesses will be back, probably blow the whole island up, too. We should go!"

They set off through the ruins, the old woman and her machine leading, Westerly walking beside Nathan. "You were lucky to find us," he told the Arcadian.

"Oh, I knew where you were. You were heading in this direction when you set off the bees, and I knew about her bolthole in those ruins. She'd been there before, after we came, and perhaps she was thinking of hiding from us when time came to leave. Though until you arrived, I didn't think she'd have the courage to try and escape." He smiled. "Floyd was real mad about the bees; he couldn't shoot *them* down with that pistol, though he burned down the hives. Got stung for his pains, too. Swore he'd cut up both of you."

"But you didn't tell him where we were."

"I was kind of relieved when you escaped. Things were getting out of hand even then; I guess maybe I should have done more." He knuckled his eyes, reset his steel-rimmed spectacles. One side of his face was scorched; holes were charred in his black jeans and his loose old-fashioned blouson. "It wasn't supposed to be like this. We're supposed to be a democracy. But Floyd kind of took over."

The old woman, hobbling stubbornly ahead, looked back and said, "That's what happens to all democracies, boy."

"Floyd was just a quiet kid, back home. I don't know what's gotten into him."

"It's like the ghostweed," Westerly said, struck and pleased by the parallel. He pulled loose a diaphanous handful from a bank that climbed a fallen fluxbarrier. "On Serenity, where it comes from, it grows no higher than your knees, and grows sparsely at that. Put it somewhere where there's no control, where it isn't supposed to be, and look what happens." He smiled, suddenly happy. He hadn't thought like that in years, thought about the way things were and why. He'd simply ignored the travails of human history; he'd cut himself off. Now he was back in it, and deeper than he cared to admit, but he was happy to be walking side by side with this stranger, this Earthman, as the old woman and her machine led them through the devastated circles of the launch pads.

And then the machine stopped. "Something ahead," it said. "Perhaps the discharge of your pistol, Seyour Westerly. I cannot tell exactly where; too far away."

Westerly took out the Witness's pistol and handed it to Nathan, who almost dropped it. "It's just a laser," he told the Arcadian, "no need to be nervous. Keep it hidden, all right?"

Nathan started to say something, then simply shrugged and tucked the weapon away.

"Let's go," Westerly said, and led the way out of the broken maze of the spacefield. Beyond, as he had remembered, was the broad road that circled the island, broken now, with weeds thrusting aside its tilted slabs. And beyond the road was the ocean. Its fresh breeze blew in their faces, and white sea birds rode the air overhead, calling with harsh voices.

"Raise your ship," the old woman said. She reached up with her augmented arm and tugged at her pigtail, plainly nervous in the open. "Raise it up. Tell me the signal."

Westerly looked at the machine. "A pure high C note, oscillating at ten cycles per second on one hundred and fifty megahertz."

"A simple siren song," the machine observed complacently.

"Well, do it," Catarina de Cyrene said, clutching at her black net as it fluttered in the breeze. And when nothing had happened after a minute, "Goddamn, don't tell me you can't."

"I am signalling," the machine said, "but there is no response."

"You have to be close," Westerly told her. "Otherwise anyone could have taken the transmitter from me and called up the ship for themselves. We have to walk around that bluff. Then you'll see."

Parts of the road had subsided, forming deep inlets at the bottom of which white water seethed and ebbed; the largest forced the three people and the machine to take long detours. Catarina de Cyrene wrapped a fold of black net over her white hair to protect herself from the sun; the machine kept close to her heels.

Westerly took the lead, a lightness in his head compounded of hunger and anticipatory fear. He was fairly sure that he knew who would be waiting for him, but for all his scheming he didn't quite know what would happen. Yet he had to have his ship.

The road looped around the bluff and then sloped down and vanished in a level stretch of sand. Blowing grains stung Westerly's face. He looked at the concrete embankment that backed the beach, and at the wind-twisted groves of live oak above it, then turned and gestured at the sea. "Raise it up," he told the machine.

Far out in the glittering swell, a long way beyond the shifting boundary where combers began their curling runs towards the beach, the sea rose in a long smooth hump which broke in a flurry of white as the ship came up, its curved hull and then the delta wing beneath glistening in the sunlight. Under the dumb urge of its programming, Westerly's ship turned and sped across the water towards the beach, coming to a rest a dozen metres above the beach, its triangular shadow falling across the watchers. "Goddamn," Westerly heard the old mechanic say reverentially, and then Nathan yelled a warning.

And beyond him the sea erupted in a gout of steam and foam that spouted higher than the back of the floating ship.

Nathan reached inside his blouson for the laser, but Westerly caught his arm and murmured, more calmly than he felt, "No. Wait."

One, then another, then half a dozen more: the figures rose from the edge of the embankment and dropped onto the beach. The pistol in his hand, Floyd swaggered up to Westerly, Marie and sandy-haired Iry at his back.

"Well now," Floyd said, pushing back his long fringe and squinting up at the singleship's underbelly. His bare chest and arms were dotted with puffy white blisters. "I guess you're wondering how I knew you'd be here."

"Not at all. You found out when you tortured that Witness. They had prepared an ambush here for me, and I suppose I should thank you for saving me from it."

"Pretty smart for an old man. I suppose you know what I want as well."

Westerly gestured at the ship above their heads. "You want the weapons I have in there. But I'm not all that clever, you know. I didn't realize how ruthless you were."

Floyd hefted the pistol. "Yeah, well, we don't have things like this on Earth."

"You don't have much on Earth, anymore. What about the others?"

"Oh, you can go free, when I've gotten what I want. But I want to deal with the traitor there, and the old woman." He touched his bee-stung chest.

Westerly moved then, but the machine moved faster. It smashed into Floyd's ankles and began to claw up his body as he fell. The man rolled away and staggered to his feet, backing away as the machine advanced on him. "Call it off," Floyd yelled, and swiped at it with the pistol. Westerly saw the fat blue spark, heard the flat crack of the discharge. Floyd yelped and danced back as the machine snatched at his knees with its tentacles. "Call the fucking thing off!" the Arcadian shouted, and staggered and fell, rolling backwards and coming up with the pistol at the ready. Westerly saw the look in Floyd's face and ducked just as the pistol went off.

The machine blew apart in a flare of violet, spraying molten sand and live steam and a shower of red-hot fragments. Westerly covered his face as burning stuff pattered all around; behind him one of the Arcadians grunted and clutched the place where something had gouged a chunk from his arm.

Floyd lay face down beyond the fused crater, the pistol still clutched in his outstretched hand. A halo of red soaked into the sand around his head. Before anyone else thought to move Westerly jumped the crater, jarring his wounded thigh, pried loose the pistol and felt for a pulse. His hand came away sticky with blood.

"How is he?" Nathan was training the laser on the other Arcadians, his face entirely white except for the livid burn on his cheek.

"Dead." Westerly was trembling, not with the residue of fear (he was still afraid), but with an almost irresistible urge to laugh. He walked over to Floyd's lieutenants and said as steadily as he could, "You two have no quarrel with me, but you'll have to answer to your own people." He looked at the rest of the Arcadians. "What about all of you? Is it over?"

"We never wanted trouble," Marie said, biting her lip. She dropped her heavy rifle on the sand, and one by one the others copied her.

Catarina de Cyrene knelt over the steaming crater, then straightened with the machine's sensor-cluster held in the hand of her augmented arm like a flower. The net bunched above the manipulators was smouldering. She looked at Westerly and said, "You knew what we were walking into. You should have told me, singleship pilot."

"Why do you think I gave Nathan the laser? Besides, you wouldn't have come with me if you'd known." Westerly turned to Marie and asked, "Are any of the Witnesses left alive?"

"One," she admitted quietly; Westerly told her to bring the prisoner down.

The Witness was a small, bright-eyed man in voluminous particoloured clothes that fluttered around him as he stepped cockily down the beach. He glanced at Floyd's body and at the pistol Westerly held, and shrugged. "We needed your ship," was his only explanation, and when Westerly said that he'd known that all along, the little man seemed amused. "Who told you? One of our people?"

"In a way. Some of the bodyguards tried to stop the ones who shot me down, and when they failed, they fled in the direction of your telescopes. I figured they were in your employ."

"A pity you couldn't have hired more reliable people. Being

shot down was your saving." He was looking up at the belly of the ship. "Tell me, how did you call it out of the sea?"

"A radio signal."

"Ah. How quaintly simple. The question always was, what sort of signal, and what else besides. That's why we waited for you here. We weren't sure if you'd booby-trapped it. Otherwise—"

"Otherwise you'd have killed me as soon as I'd given you Bifrost's location. Tell me, how did you know the ship was hidden here?"

"We had agents all along the coast. We knew you'd have to land fairly close to where we'd arranged to meet you."

"The fisherman."

"Yes, he was a fisherman, the man who spotted you."

Westerly laughed. "Your help wasn't too reliable, either. After I was shot down, your fisherman helped me across to the island then robbed me."

"Thank you for telling me. He will be dealt with in due course."

"What makes you think I'm going to let you go?"

"Why else would you want to talk with me?" the little man asked, folding his arms calmly. "Besides, do not think I am afraid of death. I am already elevated sixty degrees within the immanence of the living Godhead. I have logged over a hundred hours of prayer."

"Your prayers won't reach the Gods for thousands of years yet. If they are Gods. And if they're listening."

"Oh, I will not argue with you—"

"That's wise," Catarina de Cyrene said. "You'd save a lot of breath otherwise wasted to no purpose. He listens only to himself." She flung away the sensor-cluster and turned her back on Westerly.

The Witness raised an eyebrow, then resumed his little speech as if nothing had happened. "We no longer need to proselytize; that is one reason why my sect will retreat to the world you discovered. When our petitions are answered, we will have to deal with you colonists; until then, we will leave you be."

"Thank you," Westerly said dryly. "Now, go back and tell your people I won't betray the location of Bifrost. You needn't kill me."

The little man looked at the Arcadians, then mockingly bowed to Westerly and started up the curve of the beach.

Watching, Nathan said, "We must leave, too. Or they will take their revenge on us."

"I don't think so," Westerly said. "But in case – here." He handed over his pistol.

Nathan took it gingerly and stared at Westerly for a few moments, his eyes hidden behind his spectacles. Then, a weapon in either hand, he walked out of the shadow of the hanging ship to the edge of the sea and threw both pistols a long way out into the water. When he came back, Westerly said, "You're crazy. Those would help your people survive."

"No. We would fight over them and destroy ourselves, or we would destroy others with them." Nathan scratched under his beard. "You know, Mister Westerly, you are a little like a God, coming from the sky and changing our lives. Perhaps it is as well Earth no longer bothers with the stars. Good luck to you, anyway."

He spoke to the other Arcadians, had them pick up Floyd's body. When it was turned over to show the shattered bloody face, Iry said, "*Jesus Christ*," and vomited convulsively into his hands. Trembling, Marie wrapped an arm around his waist, and together they followed the others up the beach, climbing onto the ruined road and turning out of sight beyond the stunted live oaks.

Westerly went up to the old woman, but didn't quite dare touch her. "I promised I'd take you away," he said, "and I'll hold to that. And I'm sorry about your machine. I didn't mean for it to happen like that."

She turned. Her eyes, sunken in her wrinkled face, glittered. "I don't think you're sorry. I might have known; you singleship pilots care for nothing but yourselves." She held up the clawed hand of her augmented arm when Westerly began to speak. "No, I'm not going with you. Can you imagine me out there? No, the other mechanics lived out their lives here, and so can I. Only there'll be no one to bury my bones, if that makes a difference. Leave Earth to its heirs, singleship pilot." She gathered her ragged net around herself and added, almost shyly, "I suppose yours is the last starship I'll ever see, and I'd like to watch it go up. Is it safe to stay here when you lift?"

"I'll go up just like an elevator. You won't have a hair on your head disturbed." He ordered the ship to let down its ladder and ascended, not looking back even when the old mechanic shouted after him.

As he had promised, he took the ship up straight and level, the island falling away on the screen, a detail lost in the ragged shore that was itself lost in the great blue curve of the planet. And he felt a sudden empty yearning as he rose above it all, as if he, too, could find no better way to end his years than on the shore of Earth, at Galveston, instead of fleeing into emptiness with only his life and his ship and, still hidden in the heel of his left boot, the price of a world. And with Catarina de Cyrene's last words, the words he would puzzle over the rest of his long, long life in the worlds above: *You're dead to reality up there; you should hope the Witnesses can call up their Gods after all.*

A few weak, old man's tears pricked Westerly's eyes, swelling but not falling in the negligible pull of the ship's acceleration. When he had wiped them away, the ship had already turned on the first stage of its programmed course. On the screen now were only stars. Westerly didn't bother to look back.